CYANIDE

Library of Congress Control Number:		2016901718
ISBN:	Hardcover	978-1-5144-5625-5
	Softcover	978-1-5144-5624-8
	eBook	978-1-5144-5623-1

Print information available on the last page.

Rev. date: 09/30/2016

To order additional copies of this book, contact:
Xlibris
1-888-795-4274
www.Xlibris.com
Orders@Xlibris.com
732111

First and foremost, I like to thank God, my family, all my closes friends and the many who read this book. Life only comes around once. So enjoy it and cherish it every day, because it is not promised tomorrow.

SYRIA

Around the year 2014 over the Syrian border, there was a small town named Kobani. A terrorist group had stormed the town, terrorizing and killing all who went against their belief and faith. Those who didn't convert to their law were forced to pay fines or face death and die by the sword. In a community of small residential stone buildings under siege, rebel fighters hid from aerial bombings coming from the US, Saudi, and Russian coalitions. In the center of town inside a tiny second-floor apartment was a young militant fighter by the name of Yousef Azaan. The twenty-year-old Syrian rebel was on his computer, chatting with a fifteen-year-old Muslim female by the name of Avesta Namara from the United States. For the last few weeks, he had been trying to convince her and a dozen other young females around the world who would fall into his propaganda and travel to Syria to support his brother fighters. He went on to text her, "And you can become a wife of a jihadist bearing his children and continue to spread the word of our God. And if your husband dies in combat, you will become the wife of a martyr." The young Brooklyn native girl seemed intrigued when Yousef sent her a picture of an AK-47 with the promise of it being hers if she took the long journey. After she got off line, she went to bed thinking, and she was interested in the adventure of marrying a militant fighter and running off to join him in the Holy War.

In Syria, bombs were heard around the neighboring villages, pounding the streets of Kobani as the skies lit up and smoke filled the surrounding air from shell artillery. A group of Syrian fighters armed with AK-47s and rocket launchers hid inside Yousef's building as a US F-15 fighter jet flew over them, dropping a five-hundred-pound bomb. The explosion pulverized the small residential building, leaving concrete rubble and countless human body parts scattered all over the place. Yousef was blown to pieces. The upper part of his body, which was still intact was hovering over the computer he was on before the fatal blast.

A few miles down the road, there was a group of militant women fighters of mixed nationalities dressed in all-black, full-length garments called burkas with their faces covered in a veil that stormed a house and held a Kurdish family at gunpoint. They ordered the mother and father to lie on the floor and told their two teenage daughters to get up from their beds. As they were dragged out of thier house, their father was shot trying to stop the abduction. His wife went over to help him; screaming hysterically, she kneeled down next to him and watched him die in her arms. The militant woman acting under the orders of a high-level leader of a radical terrorist group led the abducted teens into a van that was full of other young frightened girls held against their will. The van drove alongside a dirt trail into the outskirts of the town. They stopped at a house and unloaded the innocent, terrified girls. The militant women took them inside a house where it was full of drunk rebel fighters from all over the world.

They were told by one of the militant woman, "This is your reward for fighting against our enemies. These young women are ready to bear your children, to help grow our army, to reform, and to caliphate all the states in the Middle East. And death will come to those who stand in our path!"

The men started to scream and cheer. Each one of them grabbed one of the young girls, took them into separate rooms, and repeatedly raped them.

Yousef's father was frantically looking for his son. He saw him lying dead, blown in half and still clutching onto his computer. "Rest in peace, my son. You're now with God." He grabbed the hard drive that was covered in blood and placed a blanket over what was left of his son's body.`

Yemen

An old Yemen man roughly in his sixties by the name of Maureen Khalil and his twenty-one-year old son Arif Khalil were riding on camels across the Yemen border into Saudi Arabia. They stopped at a Saudi checkpoint and gave the guards 375.11 riyal, the equivalent of one hundred US dollars to let them cross into Saudi Arabia. They then proceeded to ride there camels alongside a interstate highway in the middle of the night. A young Arab by the name of Hakeem was driving toward the Yemeni men in his GTO Ferrari. Finally, Hakeem see's two men sitting on their camels on the side of the road a few hundred feet away. The speedometer on the G.T.O read one hundred fifty miles an hour. He gradually slows down, and stepped out his shiny red car. He went over to the passenger side and pulled out a young Arabian female whose hands were tied together. The old Yemeni and his son jumped off their camels to greet and hug Hakeem. He told Marudeen in Arabic, "Long time don't see. I told you I wasn't going to fail you."

"Thank you. This will not be forgotten." They went over to the female who was standing by the side of the car. Then the old man pulled out a syringe with a white substance in it. Arif grabbed the frighten girl and held her arm out.

She started to scream, "What are you doing? Let me go!" Marudeen stuck her with a needle full of a poisonous substance he created from a dangerous mixture of toxic chemicals into a vein on her right arm. Then they all watched as she dropped to the floor and started to shake, while foam came out heavily from her mouth. As she was moaning in Arabic "Please help me, my eyes they burning, my throat, my mouth, my ears are burning, what the hell you stuck me with? Help me!" She started to shake, bleeding out her nose, eyes, mouth and ears, as she was screaming, "Help me! Please help me!" She got up and ran toward Hakeem who ran away from her, frightened. Then she fell to the ground as her body started to shake violently; her bleeding eyes popped out from her head and rolled toward Marudeen's feet. He kicked her pupils down the road and laughed as he watched her die.

Hakeem stared in disbelief. "Wow, what a violent way to die. The infidels of America, brace yourself for what's coming." He went into his trunk, pulled out a bag full of money, and told Marudeen, "This is more than enough to fund the trip round way for your nephew Abdul."

Marudeen hugged him, "Thank you. Now everything is in motion. I will keep you informed." Marudeen and his son got back on their camels and headed back to Yemen.

Brooklyn, New York

Abdul Malik was a twenty-four year old Yemenis native who was a self radicalized extremist. His parents migrated to the United States in the early nineties. When Abdul was a teen he ran away from home. His parents did not want no part of his sudden disturbing behavior and threatened to send him back to Yemen. A few years later he married and had two boys. He was walking with his four cousins Usman Mohammed, Rahan Abouhamed, Zyan Alijaber, and Agar Nasar. They walked by the Barclay's Center located in downtown Brooklyn, New York. Mohammed told his cousin, "You know, Abdul, I would love to blow up that building one day."

"I have a better plan."

Rehan asked him, "What plan?"

"My uncle from the other side wants me to travel to him to inform me better."

Mohammed asked, "Can I go? It would be an honor to help carry out any mission to destroy these American snakes."

"No, it is best you stay here and watch over our family for it is a long journey to our homeland back in Yemen. But I assure you once I return, you will help carry out a plan that would make 9/11 look like kids work."

Rahan said, "At your request, I'm here faithfully.

Mohammad added, "And I'm here for you till death."

Nasar agreed, "Any place, anywhere, anytime, my sword will be ready.

Abdul laughed. "You mean your AK-47."

Zyan put a fist in the air. "So will mine."

Abdul grabbed Zyan's hand, "I know you been anxiously waiting for your turn to fight the crusaders, and it will come. We must be careful and stay under the radar. Once our mission is completed, we can claim victory."

"How long before that happens?"

"Sooner than you could imagine."

"Just give me the green light. Abdul, there are other effective ways for me as a lone wolf, as they call us, to ram a truck into a crowded city street in Times Square or storm into a department store with my AK-47 with a thousand rounds and cause destruction."

"Relax, my young warrior, your time will come to join your brothers in the battlefields or cause havoc here."

"I want to go to Syria and join my fellow brothers. Abdul, will you come?" Rahan asked.

Abdul put his hand on his shoulder, "No, my brother, they are fighting out there for a different cause than what I was raised to believe in. They are killing each other for one ruler who evidently wants to unite Syria and Iraq together as one Islamic state at any human cost. I have my own agenda. Now let's go inside and pray." They all entered the mosque.

Zyan saw his school friend Iman Binhagi and gave him a hug. He told him, "We must talk later. It is important you join our brotherhood." From the other side of the mosque Iman's father Farhan grinned when he saw his son having a conversation with Zyan.

Over at the Binhagi household, Fariah Binhagi and her fifteen-year-old daughter Asma were folding clothes. "Here, Asma, put these socks in the drawer." Asma grabbed the socks and asked her mother about a new trend of young Muslim girls leaving to fight in Syria. "Asma, your father and your brother Iman were talking about that earlier. When young Muslim girls amused the thought of going off to the Middle East to join radical fighters, they are drawn to the idea of supporting their so-called brothers and sisters to support them, even having jihadist children to continue their caliphate agenda."

"But mother, so many girls are just getting up and leaving. Not just here but all over the world. Maybe they are not happy at home or feel like they don't fit into the Western society."

"Asma, where they want to go makes here look like paradise. These young women are becoming radicalized, traveling to the Middle East without their parents' consent. Many of these teenage girls via the Internet make contact with these foolish extremist who paint a picture of being warriors of war, please. To these girls, it seems like an adventure. They are young and naive. They don't understand the conflict or their faith and are easily manipulated. There is a civil war going on there where Sunni's are fighting and attacking other Shia Muslims, innocent Christians, and Jews, massacres led by people with evil intentions. Marry a doctor and bare his children and not of a jihadist who wants to put his kids' life in the battlefields or raise them to hate and kill. I will never approve of you marrying an extremist, do you hear me, Asma?"

"Yes, I do, Mother."

Bronx, New York

Julio Mendez a.k.a. Who, was a drug dealer well connected in the drug trade. He was a twenty-five-year old Puerto Rican native born and raised in the Bronx. He was closely associated with a sophisticated international drug smuggling organization named Los Hermnanos Fuerte which means "strong brothers." One sunny afternoon, he was walking up the block with his pit bull he named Killer. He was listening to hip hop on his wireless headphones. Julio walked by a line of addicts who were waiting to go inside a building to buy crack and powdered cocaine. Two blocks away, a drug task force team composed of four cars were lined up behind each other. Capt. John Trevor from the Bronx Task Force was the commander in charge of a buy and bust operation. Two members of his team, undercover Agent John Romo and his partner Agent Ryan Muller were walking toward a building where drugs were being sold. Agent Muller's role was to watch his partner's back as he brought drugs and safely left the drug location. After the drugs were purchased, Muller was to stay behind to watch where the buy-bust money went. Jessica Riley, a twenty-seven-year-old female officer was assigned to the Drug Task Force K-9 Division Department. She'd been working with Sammy, a four-year-old K-9 German Shepherd for the last two years in the Narcotics Department. She was in an unmarked truck, patting Sammy. "You ready to go to work, big boy?"

Julio made his way into the building with his dog Killer. The all black two-year-old Gator pit bull was wearing a matching gold chain like his owner. There was a crackhead smoking crack under the staircase. Julio got furious and ordered Killer to attack the addict. Julio screamed at the crack head, "What the fuck. I told ya, fucking crack heads, no smoking in the building!"

The drug addict started crying, "Please hold your dog! I'm sorry! Don't let him bite me. I got AIDS!." As the addict ran out the building, Killer ran behind him and bit a hole in the back of his dirty pants, showing the crack of the fiend's ass. Julio screamed at Killer to come back to him. The dog ran back to his master.

Julio patted Killer on the head. "Good boy."

About ten customers along with the two undercover agents were walking up the stairs to buy drugs. Agent Muller walked by Julio and onto the third floor, where he stopped and looked down to the second floor as he watched his partner put in a folded one-hundred-dollar bill into a whole in apartment door number 2. He asked for three crack bottles of red tops and two bags of cocaine. When Romo was in possession of the drugs and left, Muller radioed in, "The hawk has landed."

Captain Trevor radioed in to his team, "It's a go. Roll in!" All four unmarked cars sped toward the drug location.

Julio knocked on apartment door number 2. A teenage girl by the name of Rosa looked through the peep hole and opened the door. "Hey, what's up boo, you coming in?"

"Na." She hands him a bag full of money. "Why you don't like coming in?" Julio handed her a book bag full of drugs.

"Shit too hot around here. When you get off work later on, hit me up so we go somewhere and smoke something, cool?"

Killer started to bark toward the third floor. Julio looked up and saw the undercover agent. "Who the fuck is that?" He let his dog loose. Killer ran up the stairs, charging toward the undercover agent. Muller pulled out his gun and fired one round at Killer but missed. The bullet ricocheted and went into an apartment on the third floor. A two-year-old baby ran when he saw a rat jumping in the air. Apparently, the rodent was hit by the cop's stray bullet. Outside in the hallway, Killer, the vicious pit bull was biting Agent Muller on the arm, causing him to drop his weapon, which had fell down the stairs. When Julio heard the gunshot, he ran down the stairs but saw a few undercover agents running up the stairs toward him. "O, shit!" He ran back up the stairs. He saw Muller's weapon on the side of the steps and picked it up. Killer was on top of the officer, biting him on the leg. Julio told his dog, "Good boy, good boy, get him!"

The task force had heard a gunshot and were racing up the stairs. Jessica released the K-9 and when Sammy reached the third floor, it started to fight with Killer. Julio was running up toward the roof. He called Killer, which ran up the stairs. Jessica and the K-9 ran up the stairs behind Julio and Killer as the other agents were kicking down the door to the second-floor apartment. Agents from the Bronx Task Force stormed in the house, and more gunfire was being heard echoing through the six-story hallway

building. Officers were firing their weapons at a suspect who was shooting back at them as he was climbing out the fire escape. He then jumped two stories down onto a bunch of garbage bags, shooting at agents who were covering the back of the building. He was shot dead. Upstairs, Rosa was in the bathroom trying to flush a large quantity of drugs down the toilet. Officers kicked in the bathroom door and placed her in handcuffs along with another girl who was in a back room under a bed. When Jessica reached the roof of the building, she had her gun drawn. As she slowly opened the door to the roof, Killer charged toward her. She let off one round that struck Killer in the chest, killing the dog instantly.

Julio ran and jumped from one roof to another as Jessica and Sammy were in pursuit. When the K-9 had Julio cornered, he let off one round, shooting Sammy in the left eye.

"That's for Killer you stinking mutt!" Jessica who was jumping the rooftop and shooting at Julio was screaming, "No!"

Julio shot back at her. When she landed, she fell to the ground bleeding from the side of her head from a gunshot wound. Julio kept running, jumping rooftop after rooftop. Captain Trevor and Agent Muller arrived to where Jessica was lying unconscious, bleeding to death. Blood was gushing from the side of her head. Trevor pressed his hat against the hole to stop the bleeding. Captain Trevor was screaming on his radio for an ambulance. Muller kept going after Julio. As Captain Trevor was holding Jessica in his arms, he was saying, "Please, Jes, hold on. Don't die on me. Don't die on me!"

Julio was running down the stairs of a building with Muller in pursuit. There was a tenet coming up the stairs with a shopping cart full of food. Julio jumped a whole stair case to the next landing, knocking the old man down and pushing him hard to get out of his way. The old man threw a tomato at Julio, screaming, "You mother fucker!"

Muller ran past the old man and slipped on the tomato, falling to the first-floor landing. Julio emerged from the bottom of the stairs and said in Spanish, "Fucking pig!" He shot the undercover agent in the neck and lower back then ran out the building.

It was a sunny day, kids were outside playing in the water that was coming from an open pump on the sidewalk. Across the street, there was a young kid cleaning his dirt bike. He turned it on and started to rev the engine. Julio came from behind and pushed the kid so hard toward the running pump that the force of the water forced him onto the middle of the street. A car was coming and saw the kid lying there. The driver tried to stop but lost control, narrowly missing him and crashing onto other

parked cars. Julio hopped on the dirt bike and raced off, doing a wheelie and passing a police car that was on the way to the crime scene.

Ken Riley was a police officer for the NYPD who'd been on the force for two years. He just turned thirty years old. He was fairly built, six-feet tall and came from a mixed family who were half Irish and Italian. He was on his way to work when he heard over his radio that two undercover cops were shot in a drug raid. Then he got a call confirming it was his sister Jessica who got shot. He rushed over to the hospital where he saw Captain Trevor, Jessica's superior in the emergency room.

He briefed Ken on his sister's condition. "She's in a coma from a gunshot wound to the head. She had to get emergency surgery."

Ken asked the captain, "how bad is it?"

"The bullet entered the side of her head and exited through the top. She lost a lot of blood. We are all praying she pulls through. She's a tough girl." Ken saw his father and mother entering the emergency room.

Ken's mother Gloria asked him, "How is she? Is my baby going to be all right?"

"They operating on her now."

"Where was she shot?" Kens father Henry asked.

"In the head." Gloria started to cry out loud.

Henry hugged her. "She's going to pull through. Don't worry."

Ken told his family he was going to find out who did that to his sister. He pulled John to the side and asked him if he could transfer over to his division. Ken wanted to bring down the drug gang that shot his sister. John told him to stop by his office in the morning.

Three hours later, Dr. Stanley Evans briefed the Riley family on Jessica's condition. He stated, "Due to the amount of blood she had lost, Jessica had slipped into a coma. We did manage to remove bullet fragments from her skull, and she was clear of any infections."

Ken asked the doctor, "Is she going to make it?"

"She is breathing on her own. Anytime there's a gunshot wound to the head, we take it very seriously. She's not brain dead, but brain damage is our concern. She's resting now. You could see her if you wish."

Henry told the doctor thank you. Ken and his parents entered the recovery room where Jessica was sleeping. Ken started to cry when he saw his sister lying there with tubes coming out of her mouth and a white bandage that covered her head. Ken grabbed Jessica's hand. He told her he was going to find out who shot her if it was the last thing he did on this Earth. He started to think when they were kids playing in the park. She loved when he would ride her on the back of his dirt bike doing tricks. He

prayed to God, "God, please, I never ask for much, but I'm asking you now. Please watch over my sister. Please don't let her die . . ." Henry had to take Gloria out the room because she started to cry. Captain Trevor was talking to a surgeon who operated on Agent Muller. The doctor said Trevor Muller was on a respirator on life support.

He asked, "Does that mean he is brain dead, doctor?"

She replied, "she's unresponsive."

MANHATTAN, NEW YORK CITY

The next day over at the precinct, Captain Trevor was in an investigating room sitting down in front of a two-way mirror. On the other side of the mirror, Rosa Fuentes was sitting with her head down on the table.

Officer Romeo came in with a folder tucked under his right shoulder. His left hand was covered in a bandage from Killer's bite. He put the folder on the table. Then he sat down and started to read Rosa's rap sheet. "Let's see here. Possession with intent to sell heroin, gets bailed out, case dismissed. Possession to distribute cocaine, makes bail, pleas out to a misdemeanor, and annoyed you with twenty days community service. Did you break a sweat? Possession of crack cocaine makes bail, pleas out to a misdemeanor. Oh now, it's getting interesting. Possession of a fire arm, but it was dismissed for illegal search. Assault in the second degree for slashing a girl's face. The victim never showed up to court, again dismissed. All this shit, and you just nineteen years old and never did a day in jail. But now, you fucked up. Because we got two cops in critical condition fighting for their lives, and you better pray to God those officers pull through because if they don't, everybody in that apartment is going to be charged for those officers' lives. And let's not forget criminal sale and possession of drugs and weapons charges. So if you don't want to spend the rest of your young miserable life in jail, you better start talking now."

Rosa smirked. "What do you want to know, officer?"

"Well, for starters, who was that punk who gave you the bag full of drugs when you opened the door?"

"Can I get a cigarette?" Agent Romo took out a cigarette and handed it to her. She put it in her mouth, and Romo lit it for her.

She took a long pull then Romo screamed, "Well, who the fuck is he!"

Rosa took another long pull and blew the smoke in Romo's face. "I don't know what you talking about. Now get the fuck out of here and don't come back without my lawyer, you fucking pig!"

Romo smacked Rosa in the face then left the room.

Captain Trevor told Romo, "I see you didn't get much out of her." A correction officer took her back to a holding cell.

Julio and Cisco were in Will's house playing pool. They were childhood friends who were selling drugs in the neighborhood since they were kids. Julio was the oldest out of the three. Cisco was the youngest, he was 21 and Will was 23 years old. Will's girlfriend Candy was serving the guys drinks from the bar. Will took out a few hundred dollar bills from his pocket and told Candy, "Listen babe, why don't you take the car and go shopping. Go to Victoria's Secret and bring back something sexy so you could model it for me later on tonight."

"Sure, can I get that purse you promised me?"

Will gave her a kiss. "Get whatever you want, baby girl." She grabbed the keys to the car and left the house.

Julio told Will, "Wow, she must cost you a fortune."

Will laughed. "Of course, something sexy like that is going to cost."

A correction officer stopped in front of a cell full of detainees and called out Rosa Fuente's name.

Rosa yelled, "Right here!"

"You getting bailed out."

Rosa left out the Down Town Federal Court House. She made a call on a street phone.

Julio said, "Nine ball corner pocket," and made the shot. His phone rang. He answered it, "Yo."

Rosa was on the other line, "Hey, boo, I'm out."

"Where you calling me from?"

"A street phone."

"Okay, take a cab to 569 Randall Avenue."

Will asked Julio, "Why you bringing her here? I don't know if that bitch snitching. She know a lot about us. If one of them pigs die, they going to put mad pressure on her."

Cisco added, "Yea, Julio, I don't trust no bitch."

Julio replied, "So what you want me to do, kill her?"

Will said, "Is either that or see her on the stand."

After the game was over, Julio looked out the window and saw a cab outside with Rosa in it. He sent Cisco to go and pay the cab. When Rosa came in, she hugged Julio. "I'm happy to be out of there."

Julio asked her, "Did they ask you anything?"

"What you think? They want to know who shot those two cops."

"And what you said?"

"What you think I told them, to go to hell. Hey, I'm hungry. Will, you got anything to eat? Order some pizza or something." She was sitting down on a sofa when Julio came from behind and started to strangle her with his belt. She started to foam out her mouth trying to blurt out, "I didn't snitch." She died from strangulation.

Will asked, "What you going to do with her now?"

Julio told Cisco to put her in the bathtub and fill it up with acid.

Santo Domingo

Juan Carlos Santos was living the good life. He was at his multimillion-dollar mansion in an upscale neighborhood in Santo Domingo. He was sitting by the pool smoking a cigar, listening to music, and enjoying the weather, surrounded by a group of beautiful Latin women catering to his every need. One of them was by his side waving a huge palm up and down, keeping him cool. Another one was standing behind him, giving him a neck massage and sitting on the floor was another woman giving him a pedicure.

Juan Carlos was a Dominican native in his mid-thirties. He liked to work out and loved to dance. He was born and raised in the Dominican Republic. Raised by a poor, hard-working family, Juan Carlos grew up in a small town called Moca. Both his parents died of cancer. First his father then his mother passed away when he was ten years old. His uncle Miguel was a baker and worked in a bakeshop near their home. He raised Juan Carlos who was a lonely child and took him to work after school to show him how to bake cakes and pies. Juan Carlos used to watch all the local drug dealers with their fancy cars and pretty women passing by the bakery shop. He told his uncle, "I want to be like them when I grow up."

"No, Juansito, those guys either wind up dead or in prison."

But Juan Carlos had other plans as he was growing up. He started hustling on the streets to buy expensive clothes and to keep money in his pockets, always hanging out in night clubs and dancing his pants off on the weekends. Then one night, he got lucky when he met a Colombian by the name of Diego, who was on vacation from Colombia. Diego was at a local club partying and was surrounded by beautiful women.

Juan Carlos told his friend, "You see that guy over there with all them sexy girls around him? He looks like he getting it. Money rules. Money is power."

That night, a few thugs tried to rob Diego who was coming out of the club drunk. But Juan Carlos intervened, preventing him from getting robbed. He won the heart of Diego whose brother was a drug kingpin back in Colombia. Juan Carlos flew back to Colombia with Diego, who introduced him to his brother Jose Luis Rios, an international and ruthless drug lord. That day, Juan's life changed forever. He moved up in the drug trade quickly. He always told himself with a good plug and a way to get the drugs to the States, he was going to go far in this business. He knew only smart and lucky people survived the drug game that was brutal and vicious. Right away, he won the trust of his Colombian friends, and in a blink of an eye, there he was, living a poor man's dream. He stared from the bottom and rose to the top. "Trust no one, and only a fool parts ways from his money" was what he told himself quite often in front of the mirror. Juan Carlos blew smoke in the air from a cigar he was smoking.

A young pretty maid brought him a piña colada. He told his top, trusted lieutenants Goldo and Sapo, "When I was small, I had to go outside to the back of the house like a dog to take a piss or a shit because there was no bathroom in my house. Sometimes there was no toilet paper because we couldn't afford it. Now I have ten bathrooms, and I could wipe my hairy ass with hundred-dollar bills if I want."

There were a few men with automatic machine guns patrolling the perimeter of his estate. Juan Carlos surrounded himself with loyal men. He was the leader of a Dominican Drug Gang he named Los Hermanos Ferte, which meant "strong brothers." He secured a direct pipeline with the Colombian drug cartel called the Bandidos. Juan Carlos and his gang were responsible for supplying the entire East Coast from Miami all the way up to New York, generating tens of millions of dollars annually.

COLOMBIA

Juan Carlos got on his satellite phone and contacted Jose Luis Rio's, the leader of the Colombian drug cartel, The Bandidos. Jose Luis was walking in his backyard, holding the hand of a monkey he named Mono that was dressed just like him with the same matching cowboy hat. He was on the phone discussing further shipments with Juan Carlos who had an idea on how to smuggle large amounts of money without detection back to Colombia.

Juan Carlos told Jose Luis in Spanish, "amigo, gold is the way to go. The American dollar is not even worth twenty percent on a peso. Gold is better. Your money will only grow or stay steady at thirteen hundred an ounce. Plus with my plan on how to get you the gold is better than paying crooked banks ten percent to wire money over to your country undetected. That shit adds up you know. Would you like a gold stove or a gold refrigerator? Hey, how about gold animals like a lion or a cheetah, maybe a gold rooster? Hey, I even could send you a hen with golden eggs. Whatever you want, my friend."

"Okay then, send it in gold."

"It's best to keep our money out of banks so we don't have to pay no taxes. The Rico law is no joke. They take all your money then throw you in a jail to rot."

"Yea, them blood thirsty pigs, how many times we see it happen to other people. Okay, talk to you later. I see something tasty I want to eat." Juan Carlos laughed while looking at the girl who just poured him some fresh cold lemonade.

"Yea, me too." Jose Luis Rios hung up his satellite phone. He peeled a banana and gave it to his monkey Mono.

Jose Luis Rios was a forty-year-old Colombian billionaire who owned vast land and businesses in Colombia. He grew up in Tumaco, a poor small town off the Colombian Pacific Coast where his father was a farmer harvesting coca leaves for a living. His mother Juanita died of heart failure, and afterward, his father passed away due to kidney complications from drinking too much. Jose Luis had to grow up quick from a teenager to a hard-working man. Like his father, he learned how to shave the coca off the coca bushes with his bare hands. That was how he provided food on the table for his younger sister and brother. Coca leaves were high in demand since the government was cracking down on surrounding plantations. Jose Luis took the opportunity and set up shop deep in the jungles. He had a strategy once he saw government planes fumigating neighboring coca fields as well as his, destroying his crops. So he moved to the mountains of La Balsa, a tiny community of poor Afro-Colombian families near the border of Ecuador. To get to La Balsa required a ride on donkeys to a riverside port community then ride on a fast-running river.

From there, it was a two-hour hike along a narrow trail full of poisonous snakes that went into the rebels' territory. It was that type of lawless region where Jose Luis's cartel, Los Bandedoes grew there coca leaves, an area with no roads, no telephones, no sewage, and no state presence whatsoever. The cartel used the rivers to move in the chemicals needed to mulch coca into coca pasta and out to the cocaine-making labs. Also, La Balsa was a few hours walk from Ecuador through where the Bandedoes cartel could transport their cocaine by the tons. But to get huge shipments over to Juan Carlos, he would use mini submarines, submerging through the Caribbean Sea to Puerto Rico. From there, Juan Carlos would take over the route by using small fishing vessels, and the cargo would make its way up the Key West onto Miami Ports. Jose Luis had come a long way from a peasant farmer to a king living in a fortress. He loved horses and spent a lot of time on his ranch. But to keep that lifestyle, he was at constant war with rebel narco groups to keep control of the coca fields and hiding labs he used to process the pasta that converted into cocaine. Jose Luis Rios was a terrorist in his own way who was running a cocaine manufacturing and trafficking syndicate out of Colombia. He had been and fully dedicated to the violent overthrow of the democratically elected government of Colombia. He was the world's largest supplier of cocaine and had engaged in bombing, massacres, kidnappings, and other acts of violence in Colombia. He thought about what Juan Carlos was telling him over the phone about taking gold instead of money. He told himself, "I could convert my house into a golden palace."

He walked over to his stable and patted his white horse. There was a sexy Colombian woman wearing a short tank top, tight shorts, and cowboy boots. She was grooming his horse. He walked over to her, kissed her in the mouth, and grabbed her ass. Then he got on his horse with Mono jumping on behind him. They rode off into the mountains with a few armed men following behind. After twenty minutes of riding, he stopped and hopped off his horse with Mono. They walked over to a ditch where there were lots of leaves and grass. Jose bent down and pulled a thin rope attached to a wooden round door and lifted it from the ground. He climbed down a ladder onto one of many hidden underground tunnels he built. He and Mono walked down a corridor equipped with lighting and ventilation systems that led to multiple rooms where there were topless woman with masks on. They were mixing and processing coca plants, converting them into coca pasta. There were hundreds of bricks of cocaine laying everywhere with the logo stamped Cyanide and a scorpion with a double tail. Jose Luis told a worker in Spanish, "Hurry up. We need at least another two tons by tomorrow."

"As you wish, Commander." Jose Luis grabbed a woman worker by her hair and kissed her on the back of her neck then patted her on the butt. He took her to another room, threw her on a couch and started to take his pants off.

Jose Luis's wife walked out of the main house and asked one of the armed guards in Spanish, "Have you seen my husband?"

"He is out working. Do you want me to go get him?"

"It's okay." She headed over to the pool, took off her robe, and jumped in naked.

MIAMI

The South Florida Marina was alive with seafood restaurants serving up a variety of different seafood dishes and cocktail drinks to its regulars and tourist customers. It was a little past midnight. The moon was out shining brightly, overlooking the horizon with clear skies. The marina was full of multimillion-dollar luxury boats where millionaires would drive into the marina, park their foreign cars, and sail off on their yachts around the Florida coast. A blue and white vessel slowly entered the exclusive marina and docked next to three speedboat interceptors. They were jet boats capable of chopping through the water at high velocity. A short time later, a few men started unloading bricks of cocaine on to the smaller speed boats next to the vessel.

"Hurry up!" Julio said to the men unloading the drugs, "we don't have all night!" Then all of a sudden, a bright light that came from a United States Coast Guard vessel beamed on the smugglers.

Over the police vessel's loud speaker, one could hear Special DEA Agent Ken Riley screaming behind a ski mask, "This is the DEA along with the United States Coast Guards. Put your hands behind your heads! Remain where you are standing. We have the entire marina surrounded."

All of a sudden, gunfire erupts from the smuggler's vessel. The coast guard and the DEA returned fire, killing a few of Julio's men. One of the smugglers was shot by a coast guard who fell onto one of the speedboats as he was firing his automatic weapon into the sack of cocaine that burst into the air. The dead man landed on top of the drugs. Ken was firing his machine gun at Julio who returned fire from a pump shotgun. Then Julio jumped from the vessel onto one of the Interceptors and sped out of the marina. Ken was shooting towards his direction. Bullets were hitting the sacks of cocaine that were falling off the boat as Julio was fleeing. Ken radiood to a helicopter that a white and red speedboat was racing out of the marina.

Julio called Juan Carlos who was at his family's house in Santo Domingo celebrating his cousin's birthday.

Juan Carlos went outside and stood next to his white limited-edition Range Rover Autobiography. He started to yell over the phone, "What! Damn these fucking pigs! You said they chasing you, where are you heading now?"

"I'm heading up toward Boca Raton!"

"Did you pass point A yet?"

"No, I'm like ten minutes away!"

Juan Carlos told him in Spanish, "Okay, my brother, you know what to do, good luck, and may God be with you."

Ken was helping other agents round up the smugglers on to a van while other officers from the South Florida DEA Task Force finished unloading the drugs off the vessel.

A DEA Agent was flying in a coast guard helicopter, chasing Julio and screaming out on a loudspeaker, "This is the United States Coast Guards along with the DEA. Stop the boat and turn off the engine!"

Julio revs up the engine to go faster. The agent on the helicopter radioed up ahead to another coast guard cutter and advised them that the fleeing speed boat was heading toward them.

The captain of the coast guard answered back, "Don't worry. We won't let him escape."

Julio saw an underpass up ahead where people were looking down. The helicopter rode over the underpass and saw the speedboat still trying to elude them by going faster. The speedboat ran right into a coast guard cutter and came to a complete stop. The coast guard slowly approached the speedboat. The captain is talking over the loudspeaker, telling the driver of the boat to put his hands behind his head.

When agents boarded the jet boat, they only found the driver of the boat who wasn't Julio. Upon searching the boat, it was clean as a whistle. There was no drugs on the boat. Over by the underpass Julio was in a similar speed boat to the one the coast guard intercepted. He had some helpers help him unload the drugs onto a van. Julio called Juan who was dancing at his cousin's party. He went outside and Julio told him, "More than half of the shipment was lost."

Juan Carlos asked, "How much?"

"Around five hundred keys." Juan shook his head.

"What can we do but find another way. Just ship the rest out."

"Okay, boss." Julio got in a van and drove on to Interstate 95. He got off in Boca Raton and made his way up a quiet residential street, pulling up into a driveway of a modest one-story home. A young Spanish woman looked out the window and waved at Julio. The door of the garage opened, and Julio drove the van inside. The woman closed the garage door as Julio was exiting the van.

She told Julio, "Papi, I missed you" and gave him a kiss.

Julio grabbed her. "Wow baby, you looking sexy as ever." He lifted her up and put her on top of the drying machine. They started to have sex as she was hanging on to Julio with one hand around his neck and the other hand on the washing machine.

She accidentally turned it on, and it started to vibrate as Julio was banging her. She screamed, "Oh wow, I love it!"

Brooklyn, New York

Farhan Binhaji was having tea at his house with his wife Fariah and son Iman. They were a middle eastern family who migrated to the states in the early nineties. They were in front of the TV, looking at the news elaborating on the terror crises in the Middle East, where a British Jihadist fighter had just finished beheading a journalist. Farhan told his wife, "These violent extremist use religion as a cover to hide their crimes and atrocities. Their misguided actions do not represent the overwhelming majority of Muslims who emulate the pure teachings of Islam such as justice, mercy, and freedom. They going back to the seventh century where barbarism was normal."

Iman asked his father, "Don't you think they are fighting for their freedom and land?"

"If that is their reason, then why the only ones that are dying and suffering are our very own. These criminals are committing crimes against humanity and sins of God. They force evictions, daily threats of executions, and burning of places of worship including churches. Those acts of terror don't have no place in any faith. How would you feel if strangers burst through that door and held you at gunpoint and made you change your identity, your faith, your religion, and if you don't oblige, you will be slaughtered, and your sister will be taken off to be sold off as a sex slave."

Iman held his mother's hand. "So why are our brothers and sisters running off to join the many that have already left their life of comfort to a life of war?"

Farhan took a sip from his tea and told his son, "Of course, when you are being called upon to be used as a killing machine against your own kind, one must not be fooled by the propaganda in their messages. If you have to teach an idea to a roomful of people and you are not certain what they know, concreteness is the only safe language to use because it helps you construct building blocks out of peoples existing knowledge and perceptions. Extremist always build their arguments around religious perception or set of fundamental religious beliefs."

Iman shook his head. "I'm confused."

Farhan continued, "Don't worry. You're not the only one that is. Let me give you a good example. Allah is our Lord, Mohammed is our leader." Farhan picked up the Quran and went on, "The Quran is our constitution. Now they slip in, jihad is our way, martyrdom is our desire. So you see, son, if one analyze these messages, we will appreciate that most followers cannot object to any of them. They always try to come up with innovative ways to convey their message when they cannot tamper with the message itself, so they devise new propagation techniques. Many have fallen to the rederick and find themselves being manipulated, torching and terrorizing their own kind until they are killed in a battlefield they created themselves. Before they run off and join jihadi, most of these fools are just your average schmuck looking for an identity, and when they're in the battlefields, they feel they got power over others. Osama Bin Laden once said, 'What you going to ride a weak horse or a strong one.' So you having Muslims from all over the world running off to join what seems to be a powerful group that uses the social media to spread their message. They travel thousands of miles in hopes of joining a radical terror network they know are well organized and funded. Little do they know there's a bigger picture, and they are being used as a pawn."

Iman said, "Is the war ever going to end?"

Farhan stood up, holding a Quran in his hand. "What drives the most powerful terrorist organization in the world to spread a violence the world has never seen? They believe they will grow to two hundred thousand, and at the end of the Holy War, there will be only five thousand left standing who will be saved by Jesus when he comes to Jerusalem. Now how many innocent souls will perish before they are stopped?"

"Now I understand more, and I hope to address that to my friends who have a different perception when it comes to Islam."

"Yes, my son, like those brothers over at the mosque, they look young and naive."

Asma was walking home from school with her friend Avenda. They went to the same Brooklyn School and knew each other since the fourth grade. They stopped at a bodega to buy two bottles of water. Avenda told Asma she met a friend via internet who was fighting the war over in Syria. "Really?"

"Yea, he wants me to go and get involved with the movement."

"Are you crazy! What is wrong with you? Those are Jihadist fighters. All they want to do is use you, rape you, and force you to kill other Muslims."

"No, it's not like that. I'm going to take part in a humanitarian mission, and if I have to fight alongside my brothers, then I will support them."

"Avenda, listen to me, don't be so naive. Is not like you think it is. All you are going to do is get yourself raped or killed. Don't leave a land where freedom is a way of life, and you are free to do what you wish. Where you want to go, they are hypocrites."

"Oh yea, and how would you know?"

"Okay, here is one reason. The Koran says, read and learn. But why is it that they kill young Muslim girls and women when they try to educate themselves. The agenda of that barbaric army is not in the best interest of anybody but their own. They are radical leaders who are ordering the slaughtering of thousands of innocent Muslims.

Avenda grabbed her hand. "Relax, Asma, I was just thinking about it."

"Please don't go."

"Asma, don't worry. The day I decide to go, you're going to come with me."

"You're crazy. You need to go and pray for forgiveness."

"Don't you want to have an identity and help find peace among your fellow brothers and sisters?" Asma shook her head. "Yes, I want to help make a difference but not by killing our own or betraying a country that has help me and my family have a better life."

"Oh yea, what has this country done for us but abandon our homeland after they occupied it."

"Avenda, this country can't keep fighting other people's wars. And when they feel threatened, they are going to do whatever it takes to protect their citizens."

"Well, I'm going to do the same for my people and our land, whatever it takes."

Asma grabbed Avenda's hand and closed her eyes. She started to pray, "Lord, our savior, please help us understand what is right and lead us in the right path to serve you graciously."

MANHATTAN,
NEW YORK CITY

Kenny flew back to New York. He drove up to the central command office of the DEA, where he transferred to from the Manhattan Drug Task Force. He showed the armed guard his ID. The guard opened the gate and let Ken drive in. Commander Franconia, a twenty-year-old vet with the department was at his desk with a few agents sitting opposite him. He asked Ken, "Is there any new developments pertaining the Bandidos cartel?"

Ken directed everybody's attention to a screen on the wall where there was a pyramid of the Bendedoes cartel. At the top was Jose Luis Rios's face, followed by his criminal associates George Guerra, Ricardo Lopez, Fernando Garcia and Antonio Dias. Ken went on to say, "According to our contour partners in the Dominican Republic, Mr. Rios supplies a sophisticated drug gang ran by Juan Carlos Santos. That gang is responsible for smuggling tons of cocaine using the Key West throughout the last decade. There's been recent reports of lots of activity going on in and around the Caribbean Islands, using the ports of Puerto Rico as a main hub. That information was attained by a special narcotic officer posing as a double undercover agent who infiltrated the organization by working at the docks as a dock inspector. Agent Rafael Hernandez would accept large amounts of money in exchange for letting huge shipments in without being searched. Unfortunately, one to many shipments were getting intercepted, and Hernandez was found shot dead outside his house as he drove up his driveway. His undercover work led to a few indictments that resulted in sum convictions. But Juan Carlos and his connection, the Bandidos, are still at large and fully operating globally while Juan Carlos's criminal

26

enterprise is flooding the streets of Miami all the way up the East Coast. We've been busting up a lot of the cartels' stash houses and blocks where they operate, but it's like we close down one and they open five more."

A special narcotic agent by the name of Randy Parker asked Ken, "But if we know who they are, why don't we go after them?"

Commander Franconia told Randy, "It's not that easy. These thugs got the politicians and government in their pockets. We just can't go into these countries and start arresting these scumbags if the government is protecting them.

Ken said, "Well then, sir, I need to hit the streets and work on infiltrating this well organized gang."

"You have my full support, son. Use all the resources you need."

"Okay then, I need a kilo of cocaine to start selling to some of the lower drug dealers and gain their trust to work my way up the chain and a few toys, you know a nice street ride."

"Oh, you're going hard. You want a gold chain too?"

"As a matter of fact, yes, and a shiny watch too."

GEORGIA

Victor Alvarez was driving up the 95 North Thruway in a tractor trailer, hauling a half dozen luxurious SUVs. He exited on to the Georgia thruway, arriving at his first stop. For years, Juan Carlos's drug gang had been using stash cars with concealed traps full of kilos of cocaine to transport their drugs up and down the East Coast. The tractor trailer pulled up to a rest stop and unloaded a Range Rover.

Troy, a local drug dealer from Georgia, had been working for the Dominican drug gang for years. He pulled up to the rest stop, got out of his Mercedes Benz and told his girlfriend to get on the driver's side. Troy opened up the trunk and pulled out a duffel bag full of money. A white old couple pulled up in a motor home next to the tractor trailer.

Julio came out and grabbed the duffel bag from Troy. "My man, how you been?"

"I couldn't be better. The town is dry. Same shit, right?"

"Like always. Bro, it's all here?"

"Yup, all in hundos." Julio got back in the motor truck. "See you next week."

"You know it for sure." Troy went over to Victor and gave him a hug. "Yo, Vic, when are you going to come and hang out? I got a strip club full of bitches. Julio always says he coming, but he's full of shit."

"Don't worry. When you least expect it, I be walking in that strip club ready to hit everything."

Both men started to laugh. Victor put a temporary license plate on the back of the Range. He shook Troy's hand and climbed up onto his truck. Troy got in the Range Rover and drove out of the rest stop with his girlfriend following him in the Benz.

Over at Troy's comedy strip club, a guest comedian was on stage telling jokes to a local crowd. While the strippers were taking a break in-between sets, the comedian by the name of G-Man had the crowd laughing. He told the crowd, "When I heard my manager booked me to a comedy strip club, I jumped on the first plane down here. Shit, I was getting paid for telling cheesy jokes and at the end of the night, I was getting free brains. Yea, at least here they have some decent looking chicks. Shit, I remember awhile back it was my boy's birthday, and he invited me to go chill with him. The least I could've done since I forgot his birthday and forgot to get him something. Yo, let me tell you. It was the worst night of my life. I took him to some low-budget joint. The strippers, they had there looked like tyrannies and monsters. This one skinny bitch must have had her boobs done and something terribly went wrong. I mean she looked crazy. Her tits were hanging down to her stomach, and her nipples were dangling down to her knees. Out of all the niggas there, she came up on me talking about if I wanted to hump on her boobs for five dollars. I wanted to throw up. Then this six foot gorilla ran up on me, honestly, I thought she was a tyranny or something 'cus when she talked, she had this deep raspy voice. She asked me, 'Daddy, you want a lap dance?' I was like 'Oh no, sir, I mean, ma'am. I have theroposy, very weak knees. She said, 'Oh, don't worry. I can take your pain away.' So this nasty bitch started givin' me a hell dance. It wasn't even a lap dance because she had this disgusting smell. It was like a cheap perfume. It smelled more like them cheap oils them old people be selling in the corner three for a dollar."

The crowed started to laugh. Troy pulled up around the back. He called his manager Leroy to help him unload the keys out the Range Rover and into the basement. Troy pulled the backseat and there they were, looking as beautiful as ever, one hundred keys of cocaine. As they finished unloading the bricks, there was a commotion going on upstairs in the strippers' dressing room. Troy went upstairs and broke up a catfight between two strippers. It was Lady Love and Star. Apparently, they were fighting about a customer who was a heavy tipper.

Star told Troy, "This hoe always trying to steal my customers. I'm tired of her. You need to get rid of this ugly bitch!"

Lady Love answered back, "I saw him first" She kept trying to attack Star. Leroy was holding her back. Troy screamed at Lady Love and told her to control herself, or he was going to throw her out. She kept trying to get at Star. Leroy then grabbed Lady Love by the neck and started to drag her toward the back door.

She kept saying, "Get off me you fagot!" Then she spit in Leroy's face. He got mad and kicked her hard on her ass as he was pushing her out the back door. He told her, "And don't ever come back, you crazy bitch!" He slammed the door and went inside.

Lady Love was screaming, "Mother fucker, come out and fight me like a man!" She took out her cell phone and called her boyfriend. She told him she got thrown out of her job.

He said, "What!"

She answered, "No, I couldn't make no money."

"What! Don't come home!"

"Do what! You crazy bastard, you come out here and suck cock on the strip!" Lady Love hung up. "The nerve of him telling me don't come home without no money." She started walking down a quiet road with no shoes on. She tried to call a cab but had no luck. A white man rode by her slowly in an old pickup truck. He had a huge kitchen knife between his legs. He stopped next to Lady Love and she asked him, "Can I get a ride?"

He smiled with no teeth and said, "Sure, get in."

PARIS

Abdul heard a car honking the horn. He looked out the window and saw it was his cousin Mohammed. Abdul was inside saying bye to his wife Hindah and his two sons Aiman and Wali who were nine and ten years old.

Aiman told his father, "I'm going to miss you."

Abdul hugged him. "You think I'm not going to miss you too."

Wali asked, "Father, why can't I go with you?"

Abdul gave him a kiss on his forehead, "Don't you know why I named you Wali? It means to be a guardian. And that's what I want you to be to your brother and mother in my absence." Abdul turned to Hindah. He gave her a kiss and told her, "I shall be back soon."

Tears came down from her eyes as she hugged her husband. "Go in God's caring hands."

Mohammed drove him to the airport and wished him good luck. He then left the airport and headed toward his house. Abdul was aboard a commercial airline, flying over the North Atlantic Ocean. He landed in Paris and checked into a hotel. After he took a shower, he relaxed in front of the TV. The newscaster was showing rebel extremists fighting in Iraq and capturing Iraqi soldiers who refused to join the opposition. Many of the Iraqi soldiers were outnumbered and fled, abandoning their military post. The ones that were captured were savagely beaten, either shot or beheaded. The radical extremist rebels hung their chopped heads on poles and placed them around town. It was an effective method those barbaric animals used to scare and intimidate the Iraqi people, a country which was 99% Muslim, 42% Sunni and 51% Shia had been fighting each other for decades. And rebels who were Sunni felt the Shias were infidels and not real Muslims.

Abdul was looking at the TV, shaking his head in disbelief. He told himself, "Instead of killing their own kind, they should be killing all these Westerners." He turned off the television and prayed before he went to sleep. The next day, Abdul was boarding a plane to Turkey. On the plane, he put on his headphone and fell asleep listening to Arabic music. A while later, he was awakened by the people on board departing the plane.

When Abdul got off the plane, there was a car waiting for him.

"How was your flight?" a young Turkish woman by the name of Amreen asked him.

"Long. I can't wait to meet up with our fellow brothers."

Amreen was accompanied by her older brother Jamil. He hugged Abdul, "Welcome home, brother Abdul."

"Yes it feels good to be home." Jamil grabbed Abdul's luggage and placed them in the trunk of the car. They drove for hours into the middle of the night along the Syrian border. They saw thousands of refugees fleeing.

Amreen pointed to the refugees and told Abdul, "You see those poor people running for their lives, forced out of their homes, some families getting their children as young as ten years old snatched away from them and placed in camps where they are taught how to fire machine guns. At a young age, they teach them to hate Americans. 'The infidels must be killed because they are our enemies.' They brainwash these poor kids for years then ask them what they want to become when they grow up. The two choices are either a suicide bomber or a jihadi."

Abdul saw a group of Syrian men carrying plastic drums. He asked, "Why are they carrying those drums on their backs?"

Jamil told him, "Those are oil smugglers who are smuggling oil to Turkey. They are coming back to refill the barrels and sell it in the black market for less. That is the lifeline of the terror group to conquer land and murder their own for oil to fuel their armor cars they stole from the Iraqi army. The US spend billions of dollars for the Iraqi people and for what, to see all that equipment fall in the hands of these terrorist. The oil keeps the regime in control and well funded to continue their crimes against humanity."

Abdul shook his head. "But whose side are you on?"

"I am on the side of Allah. I am for peace and equality." Abdul told himself, if she only knew why I really came here for, she probably leave me in the desert. Amreen stopped the car along a mountain side. They are confronted by Syrian rebels. Abdul handed Amreen money. She gave it to one of the soldiers who gave them clearance, food, and water. Then the three continued their journey, entering Jordan, and passing through the city of Amman. There they stopped in a town called Azraq, which meant the Blue One. It was located alongside a desert road. Azraq was the only source of water in twelve thousand square kilometers of desert. They filled up gallons of water and kept driving into the hot Jordan desert, arriving in a town called Alaqabah, where it was situated on the northeastern tip of the Red Sea. There they went for a swim and prayed on the beach.

North Carolina

Victor was driving up 95 and saw the exit for North Carolina. He bore left on to the North Carolina thru way. He stopped at a rest stop. A Hummer truck pulled up with two black men inside. Roy and his partner James exited the truck. Leroy went to the back and took out a large duffel bag and walked over to the motor home. They knocked on the door.

Julio opened it and let the men in. Julio hugged them, "My peoples, how you been?"

Leroy replied, "Good man, what happened. You running behind."

Julio shook his head. "Yea, I know we been having a little problem getting the shipment in. There's only one hundred pieces."

James said, "What! That's going in a few days."

"Don't worry, my friend, more is on the way."

Leroy handed Victor the duffel bag full of money. "I hope so."

Victor unloaded a Silver Audi SUV from the tractor trailer. He then knocked on the motor home door. He told Julio, "Ready!"

Leroy and James hugged Julio as they were exiting the motor home. James told Julio, "My man, hope to see you next week and tell Juan to step it up to three hundred keys a week."

"Okay, I will. Be safe."

Victor asked the men, "You have the temp?"

James said, "Sure do."

Victor shook James and LeRoy's hands and said, "How you guys been?"

James replied, "Everything is Gucci. Oh yo, Vic, I looked into that college for your son. It has a lot of good programs. My son starts this fall. He's studying engineering."

"Oh yea that's what my son is majoring in." I'll call you this weekend."

"Okay"

Leroy put the temp on the Audi and waved goodbye to Victor. James then got in the Hummer and left the truck stop followed by Leroy. The RV pulled out the rest stop.

Julio opened the duffel bag and took out stacks of money, placing it through the money machine, starting the long process of counting five hundred thousand dollars in small bills.

JORDAN

Abdul was approaching the Jordan border after hours of traveling through a challenging terrain. Although Jordan was mostly covered by desert, it did have its mountains, forest, and rolling hills with river Valleys. As Jamil was driving, Amreen was showing Abdul Jordan's ancient sites that were carved from stone as they were passing through the land that was steeped in history and mystery, which spread across the desert land. It was a journey that followed the winding paths and footsteps of powerful pharaohs that ruled the land thousands of years ago. They stopped to eat as they watched the Muharram festival. Abdul treated himself to a plate called oozy, a rice dish cooked with minced meat and a variety of spices, carrots, peas, nuts, and grilled chicken. Amreen and Jamil had a plate called Mjadarra, a rice dish cooked with lentils topped with caramelized onions. There was a host of different festivals going on.

Jamil told Abdul, "This particular festival is called Muharram that celebrates the start of the Islamic New Year which happens on a different day of the year according to the cycle of the moon. There was a another festival going on too, the most popular one called the Jordan Rally. It's a motor car race which brings together those with the need for speed from every corner of the globe. For a few thrilling days, the festivals turn the Jordan's golden streets into a race track and a large international crowed can be seen getting their adrenaline filled."

After they ate, they crossed the Jordan border and into Saudi Arabia, heading for Yemen. Abdul asked Jamil, "Why is there no fighting in Jordan?"

"We are fortunate not to have oil."

VIRGINIA

Victor approached Virginia Beach and entered a rest stop. A hooker waved at him as she was walking toward him. She asked him, "Howdy there, cowboy, would you like to get that pecker sucked?"

Victor grinned. He looked around for the Virginia gang that was supposed to pick up a load, but he didn't see them. So he let the hooker in his truck. He told her, "Why not, did you brush your teeth?"

As she was giving him a blow job, a hard knock on his passenger side window startled him. It was the Virginia boys Tommy and Ricky, two white boys. Tommy opened the door and saw the chubby hooker.

Ricky said, "Ill. Victor, are you serious."

Victor turned red. "What, you never got a blow job from a fat girl."

Tommy said, laughing, "Yea, not from an ugly fat girl."

Victor gave the hooker a twenty-dollar bill.

She said, "Hey, it's thirty dollars."

"Oh yea, you ain't even finished." Victor gave her the other ten dollars. "Go on." She walked away. Victor unloaded the Honda Odyssey and tossed the keys to Tommy. Ricky handed Tommy a temporary Virginia license plate to put on the Odyssey.

Tommy waved to Victor and yelled, "See you next week, Vic!"

"All right, man, ya be safe."

The motor home Julio was in pulled up to the rest stop. Julio exited the motor home. He headed over to Tommy and Ricky who were laughing.

Tommy told Julio, "Hey, how are you, everything good?"

"Everything all right." Ricky hugged Julio. "You better get Victor a girl. I just caught him with a hunchback cow." All three men start laughing.

Julio asked Tommy, "Is it all there?"

Pointing at the money in the duffel bag. "Not a penny short."

"That's what I like to hear." Julio screamed at Victor, "Hey, I heard about your nasty ass!"

Victor drove off with his middle finger in the air.

New York City, Washington Heights

Ken parked his shiny red motorcycle in front of a jewelry store. He went inside and brought an eighteen-carat gold chain with a matching bracelet and a gold Audemars Peguet watch. He dropped close to sixty-five thousand on the jewelry. Kenny then rode over to his friend's clothing store. When he got there, he told his friend Peter he wanted to work there but wanted to portray like he was the owner. He explained he was going undercover to bring down a drug gang that left his sister in a coma during a drug raid.

Peter said, "wow, sorry to hear that. Whatever you want to do, I got your back. Just be careful. Your sister needs you now and so does your family. This is a dangerous thing you are doing."

"Yea, I know. Thanks for helping me."

Two females entered the store. They were looking at clothes that were on a rack. Ken told Peter, "Let me handle that." He headed over to the females and introduced himself as Johnny. "How you lovely ladies doing today? My, your hair is looking vibrant today."

Lynda blushed. "Thank you. You can thank my hairstylist."

"Is there anything I could help you with? Are you looking for anything in particular?"

"I'm just browsing around."

Ken showed Lynda a sexy blouse. "Now this here would look real sexy on you. They just arrived and they are on sale too. Hey, do you know why you should add this piece to your closet?"

"Okay, why should I?"

"If you try it on, I'll tell you."

Lynda's friend Rita told her, "It is pretty. I like the color too."

Lynda said, "Okay, Mr. Fashion Guy, I'll try it on." She went into the fitting room to try on the blouse.

Ken looked over to Peter who gave him a thumbs up.

Lynda came out the fitting room. "It fits good on me." As she was looking in the mirror, Rita agrees.

Ken told Lynda, "Wow, I knew it would look fabulous on you. You look amazing."

"Thank you."

"Now I'm going to tell you why you should add this to your collection. Not only you look good in it and it's on sale, but it also matches with your shoes."

Lynda and Rita start to laugh. "Yea, you're right. I think I'll take it." She brought it to the counter. Peter rang up the blouse over at the cash register.

Kenny told Lynda, "Be nice if you would wear it. If and when you let me call you someday, you could model it for me. Do you like motorcycles?"

"Depends, I don't like the bikes I see guys riding with their hands in the air."

Ken laughed. "You mean them outlaws that ride with the handle bars up in the air. No, baby, let me show you what I'm working with."

They all went outside and Ken showed the girls his red sports bike.

Lynda said, "Wow yea, I like that."

"I don't know. I think you going to stop a lot of traffic with that big booty back there."

Rita laughed and said, "Well, ain't that the point of it all."

They all started to laugh. Lynda and Ken exchanged numbers. Ken told her he was going to call her after he closed his store.

Lynda's friend said, "That's your store?"

She looked at Lynda. "Now why I ain't come in here and buy a blouse."

Ken laughed. "It's still not too late."

Will was on his block doing tricks on his motorcycle. He was one of Julio's top trusted lieutenants who was involved in the crews' everyday drug activities. He loved doing tricks on his bike, showing off around girls. He did an *endo*, which is a motorcycle trick when a rider pressed hard on the front brake, making the back of the bike go up in the air. He stop in front of his boy Cisco who was with his wife Tamika drinking a beer.

Cisco asked Will, "Let me holla at you for a second, bro. I got my customers from New Jersey who need two keys. But the only shit that's left is for the block."

Will got off his bike. "Let me make a call." Will called Julio who did not pick up; he shook his head. "There's nothing happing right now."

Cisco frowned. "Free money lost."

Will got back on his bike, "Come on, I want to pick up my girl. Let's go for a ride."

Cisco asked his wife, "You want to get something to eat?"

"Babe, remember we only got two hours then we got to go home. You forgot its Sunday and Rebecca can't babysit after eleven. She got school tomorrow and so does your daughter."

"Okay, it's just for a little while babe." Will, Cisco, and Tamika rode off. They stopped to pick up Will's girlfriend Candy then got on the highway, weaving in and out of traffic.

Ken called Lynda. He asked her if she wanted to get something to eat.

"Sure what you had in mind?"

"I leave that up to you."

"Well, how about shrimps and lobster tails."

"Em, that sounds good okay." He helped Pete close the store and got on his bike to pick up Lynda.

Will, Cisco, and the girls arrived at the restaurant located in City Island. There were other couples there who came on motorcycles too. Ken and Lynda arrived and sat at a table. A waiter took their order. After they ate, they headed toward the bar to get a couple of beers. Candy spotted her friend Lynda, who was also her stylist, walk by. She called out her name, "Lynda!" They hugged and Candy introduced Lynda to her friend Tamika. Then Ken got introduced to Cisco and Will.

The guys ordered drinks for themselves and the girls. They were all hanging out by the bar. Will asked Ken, "So where you from?"

"From the Bronx. I got a clothes store in the Heights called the Right Place. Ever heard of it or been there?"

Will said, "I think I been there. That's right next to the chicken spot, right?"

"Yea, on one five six and Saint Nick's." Ken invited them to go over one day, and they agreed to pass by.

After a while, the group decided to go to a motorcycle meeting across town. Cisco asked Ken if he wanted to go for a ride to the marina in Washington Heights.

Ken asked Lynda, "What do you think, you want to go?"

"I don't mind."

Ken told the guys, "Sure, lead the way."

Lynda pulled Ken to the side, "Hey, Johnny, be careful with them guys. They some wild boys. I know Candy. She comes to get her hair done at the salon where I work. She be bragging about how her man is a big-time baller."

"Really, which one?"

She pointed at Will and Cisco with her lips. "Both of them. They always together."

Ken started his 2015 BMW motorcycle.

Will came over and stared at the BMW. "Nice bike."

"Thanks."

Will started his R1 Yamaha as Candy was getting on. Tammy gets on the back of Cisco's Double R 1000 Honda. And they all sped off. On the highway, Ken told Lynda to hold on. Then he did a wheelie. Cisco smiled and he passed Ken doing a wheelie too. When they got off the highway, they were all at the light. As the light turned green, Will popped a wheelie and rode the motorcycle on the back wheel for a few blocks. Then Cisco joined Will doing a wheelie. Ken followed behind and he popped a wheelie.

Everybody in the streets were saying, "Wow look, they nice." People were taking videos with their phones as all three bikes were doing wheelie down the street with the girls hanging on. When they got to the marina, there were guys on their bikes doing tricks in the parking lot. Ken parked his bike, and Cisco and Will dropped off the girls and started doing tricks on their bikes. When Cisco and Will came back to Ken and the girls, Ken got on his bike and started to do some neat tricks.

Will told Cisco, "Yo, that dude's nice with it."

"Yea, he playing with that bike."

Afterward, when Ken came back, Will told him he was a daredevil.

"It ain't nothing. I been doing it for years." Ken invited everybody to the bar and told them drinks were on him. Teresa the bartender was Victor's girlfriend. He was the gang's driver who drove a tractor trailer which was used to distribute tons of cocaine up and down the East Coast.

When Teresa served Lynda a drink, she complimented her on how nice her hair was. "Actually, sometimes I do it myself. I run a salon. If you want to stop by one day to do your hair, here's my card."

"Really, I need a stylist. I'll call you this weekend to make an appointment."

Ken pulled Lynda to the side. "Why you socializing with these people like that?"

"What are you talking about. She's a bartender who wants me to do her hair. This is what I do to keep my business alive, I network. Besides if you didn't want me to mingle with none of these people, why you brought me here."

Baltimore

The motor home that was driving Julio up the East Coast parked at a rest stop in Baltimore. Julio was calling Victor but no answer. "Damn, I hope this dude didn't get stopped." Julio checks into a hotel next door to take a shower.

Victor was driving up 95 North, a Mustang speeds by him. Then Victor saw a state trooper on the side of the highway. When he passed by the trooper, he saw the patrol cars light go on.

"Lordy lord." The trooper passed him and pulled over the Mustang. Victor wiped his forehead. "Thank you, Lord."

When Julio got out the shower, he looked out the window and saw Victor unloading a Toyota 4 Runner. Julio went over to Victor, "Hey, why you ain't answer your phone?"

"The battery was dead."

A man screamed over at Julio, "Yo, Who!" Julio turned around and saw Trey, a husky dark man who was well built with long dreads. He was in control of the east and west side of Baltimore who served all the mid and low-level drug dealers. "Long time man, how's everything?"

Julio hugged Trey. "Wow! What you been eating man? Ukunuba, you blew up dogs."

"Na, man, this is yams and potatoes."

"Well whatever you're eating, you look like a brick house."

"Thanks, here you go, all in hundreds." He handed Julio a boxful of money. Julio took the box. Trey told him, "I call you next week. I want to double up. They loving this shit."

"For sure man I got you." He then gets in the 4 Runner and drove off.

Julio opened the door to the motor home and busted the driver of the motor home having sex with his wife in the back. Julio said, "Wo!"

The old man Walter told Julio, "What, you thought old people don't fuck."

SAUDI ARABIA

The land of the Saudi desert was vast, and it was impossible to judge distance. The intense sunlight reflecting off the sand tricks the eye into seeing things that didn't exist. One mistake made and one could vanish forever. Temperatures could exceed from 100° to 130°F and at night, dropped drastically to freezing temperatures.

Abdul was sleeping in the back of the jeep and woke up drenched in sweat. "Where are we?"

Amreen told him, "We are in the Arabian desert, approaching the city of Jeddah."

After driving for a few hours into the hot scorching desert, Abdul told Amreen, "I'm sweating to death from head to toe, and all I see is sand for miles."

"You already look like the color of a penny. Are you aware that this vast desert land is connected with the current conflict we are facing today?"

"What do you mean?"

"It's a long story."

Abdul yearned. "We got nothing but time and sand."

She turns around and started to explain, "For centuries, Saudi Arabia is ruled by the Al Saudi family which gave the country its name. The state was established around 1932 after along campaign to unify the Arabian Peninsula. Before then, the country had been no more than a undeveloped desert fought over by warring tribes and plagued by desert bandits. Many years ago, only nomadic Bedouins lived here. The al-Saud clan currently consisting of seven thousand princes has ruled the country since 1932. Presently, there are ten princes who share power and divide the wealth which they pass down to their kids. Saudi Arabia would have remained a primitive desert wasteland largely ignored by the rest of the world, except for one fact. It is sitting on a quarter of the globe's oil. This gives the Saudi ruling family enormous power. At a stroke, they can raise or lower the price of the oil by cutting or increasing their output. Saudi oil was discovered by accident in 1938. Since then, it has made the Saudi clan incredibly rich."

"Your point."

"For years, the Saudis have also funded terrorism. The US government is well aware that the Saudis have given money to Islamic charities that has in turn been used to fund violent terrorist organizations."

Jamil added, "Fifteen of the nineteen suicide bombers on September 11 were Saudis. Osama Bin Laden comes from a prominent Saudi family."

Amreen told Abdul, "Saudis fund mosques and schools in Pakistan. For example, the six thousand madrassas were built there with Saudi money, and it was in these schools that the Taliban was formed and trained. The Saudi Royal family always feared Iran's Shia Regime, particularly the emergence of a powerful Shia that ran the government in Iraq. Satirically, the Saudis put a preacher in every continent. Steadily they are succeeding in spreading Islam. They are globalizing Wahhabism and the American petrol purchases are paying for it. Even after September 11, the Wahhabi bureaucracy in Saudi Arabia continues to foster religious extremism. When bombs go off in Israel, Kenya, Indonesia, and elsewhere, the Saudi's are still the main source of terrorist money. The kingdom is an unwavering nerve center of ideology, indoctrination, incitement, and terrorist financing."

Jamil told Abdul, "In London, classes are taught via Saudi textbooks that Jews are repugnant and Christians are pigs. Children in the playgrounds are heard idolizing Bin Laden. Saudi textbooks around the globe teach ten-year-olds the whole world should convert to Islam and leave its false religions, for if they don't, their fate will be hell."

Amreen told Abdul, "And the twelve-years-olds are taught Jews and Christians are their enemies. And that gay people are perverted, filthy dogs that should be slaughtered."

"So what do you think of Saudi Arabia now?" Jamil asked Abdul.

"They're 100 percent right, Islam should rule the world."

Amreen went on to say, "No, you're 150 percent wrong. What sort of religion manifest marrying off teenage girls and murder old woman of witchcraft. The sort that flies planes into skyscrapers."

Abdul intervened and said while laughing, "My kind of people."

Amreen nodded her heads no. "They murder teenage girls for using Facebook and base its entire society on a ladder with Muslim men at the top, Muslim woman a few steps below, and everybody else somewhere in the bottom."

Abdul agreed, "I could live with that. Besides, whose side are you on?"

"I would like to be an equal opportunist and not live in oppression."

"So this is why Al-Qaeda was founded by a Saudi."

"Exactly, the Saudis, the wealthy citizens of a wealthy kingdom, are its best recruits. It is not poverty or oppression that makes them kill but wealth and privilege. This is where the opposite of true Islam originated, whose brutality has spread across the world and whose clans killed each other then killed or enslaved minority groups and then embarked on a wave of conquest that destroyed countless cultures, and left behind their seeds of hate of the wars we are left to fight today. And so in this modern day and age, you can clearly see and don't have to visit Saudi Arabia because diluted forms of it can be found everywhere from Cairo to London and from Islamabad to Los Angles. Years ago when America freed its slaves, Muslim immigrants brought back slavery, importing young girls to live as their slaves. Back when American woman won the right to vote, the ghost of Islam tread the streets in sheets that hid women's personality and mark them as property. The end game of the Arabs is to reduce the entire world to the level of Saudi Arabia, and that means eliminating outside influences in a long march of purification. Islamists know that they cannot enjoy complete dominance over their own people until their rivals in the West are obliterated, To turn Egypt and Malaysia into Saudi Arabia and to purify Saudi Arabia, the infidels' religions must be brought down to their subjugated level, and their nations replaced with proper Islamic states."

Abdul interrupted and said, "I see why not."

Amreen went on to say, "Islamic leaders are under no illusion that religion is a spiral matter. They know that it is a numbers' game. Wage enough wars, terrorize enough nations, marry enough barely post - pubescent girls, and use them to crank out babies. And intimidate or trick enough infidels into joining up as jihadist fighters, suicide bombers, or lone wolves and you win. That was how devil terrorist used our religion and took over so many territories and spread around the world, and that is how they are doing it again now."

Abdul asked, "What you're saying, Islam came out of the desert?"

"Yes, it has never left the desert. Instead it has brought the desert with it along with its codes, its deep hatreds, its constant deprivation, its deceptiveness, and its nomadic expansionism where radical Islam goes. The desert rises its tents and its insecurities. It was backward even at the time of its birth, and it has only become worse. Now a few radical extremist leaders want to rule at all cost, starting and ending with Muslim blood."

Abdul laughed. "And on another note, all these other nations across the globe, it's not in their best interest to stop the ongoing Wahabbi-Saudi hate machine for a simple reason."

"Why do you think?" Jamil asked.

Abdul went on to say, laughing out loud, "Because junkies don't talk back to their dealers. They are addicts to the Saudi oil supply!"

Jamil added, "The black gold." Jamil looked up to the sky and told his sister, "Looks like a sand storm is heading our way. Should we turn back?"

Abdul said, "No, we can't turn back. I need to get to Yemen. Can't we go around it?"

Amreen looked up at the sky. "Looks like that idea might be too late." The sky was changing and the winds were howling. As the sand storm was nearing, the unthinkable became a reality. The jeep started to overheat and stalled. The car suddenly came to a complete halt.

Abdul asked, "What now? Shit, what we going to do?"

Jamil asked his sister, "How far are we from Azzahr?"

"Maybe a few miles."

Abdul's face turned desperate. "Come on, let's walk the rest of the way!" He jumped out the car.

She screamed back at Abdul, "Abdul, wait. Get back in the car!" She exited the car to try to stop Abdul from walking away into the vicious sand storm that was heading their way.

Jamil got out the car, screaming, "Hey, wait for me!" Then suddenly, the wind whipped into a frenzy, and the air began to glow a seemingly radioactive red. Seconds later, the sky turned dark, and the three of them were fully enveloped in dust.

Abdul was screaming, "I can't see!" Jamil grabbed Abdul's hand as he held on to his sister's arm as well.

Amreen screamed, "Keep your eyes and mouth closed so you don't swallow the sand!" Thunder cracked the sky, and it began to rain mud. It was hard to breath. The sand was fine like flower and inescapable. Amreen relied on a handheld gadget global positioning system but could not see because the air surrounded them with sand. Abdul's nose was full of brown snot. His throat was dry and full of sand, making him choke. His eyes shed tears of mud that irritated them terribly. Finally, the sand storm passed them. They were full of wet sand that looked like dry mud.

Amreen looked at the GPS. "Keep walking. We are nearing Azzahr."

There they stopped, prayed, and headed toward Najran, a village alongside the Yemen border. Finally, Abdul could see the Yemeni mountains where he grew up as a child.

He screamed, "Dhamar, here we come!"

Santo Domingo

Juan Carlos is in his club called the Night Life. He was with his crew Raul, Sapo, and Goldo. They were scouting around for girls who would be potential mules to transport drugs for them back to the States. A waitress was popping a bottle of champagne for Juan Carlos over at the VIP section. Goldo was dancing meringue with a female twice his size. Raul and Sapo were laughing.

Sapo told Raul, "The bigger they are, the more drugs they could carry."

Raul was scouting around the club for young females. He would approach them by offering them drinks, and then he would flash lots of money to get their attention. He would tell them he was part owner of the club and was expanding to the States. He also told them they could make some good money with him if they wanted a new life. They all were eager to learn more. At the end of the night, the gang took a few girls to a house where they offered them a chance to join their organization and start a new career. They were promised visas to the States and a place to stay as well. They accepted because it gave them a chance to work and leave a poor-stricken country.

A chubby short old man who was a self-proclaimed surgeon entered the room. "All right, ladies, let's see them tetas. He approached one female and attempted to lift her blouse.

She grabbed his hairy hands. "Get off me you chomo."

"What, they didn't tell you I might be doing you a favor since them tits of yours are mighty small. When I'm finished with you, they going to be at least a size double D."

Goldo came in and told them that they were going to be carrying the drugs in a jell sack in their breasts.

Juanita's sister Desiree said, "You fucking crazy? I ain't doing that."

Juan Carlos came in the room and screamed, "Okay, this is what happens when you waste my time." He shot her in the back of the head. He then turned to the other females and yelled, "Is there anybody else here wasting my time and want to wind up like her? Speak now or forever hold your peace!"

New York City, Washington Heights

Cisco parked his 2015 Corvette in front of Ken's store. He saw a GTR Nissan and told himself, "Nice."

Ken was in the store with a vendor. He saw Cisco enter the store and went over to him.

"Hey, what's up? Glad you came by."

"What up, I told you I was going to stop by."

"You seen the new Gucci frames that came out?" Ken showed him the new collection.

"Yea, they dope man. I'm going to take the black ones. Nice store."

"Thanks." He showed Cisco a new pair of Gucci sneakers. He told Ken, "Wow, you going to make me buy everything up in here."

Ken showed Cisco a T-shirt that went with the sneakers. He told Cindy, a sales rep that works in the store, to put some quarters in the meter. As she walked out, Cisco was staring at her ass. "Wow, she's sexy. Yo, Johnny, that's your GTR?"

"Yea, that's my baby."

"How you do it, man? You got the car, the store, and the bike."

"Working hard, dude." Ken gave Cisco his change for the things he brought. They walked outside.

Cisco looked at the GTR and told Johnny, "I was going to get that, but instead, I got the Vet."

"Funny, I was going to get the Vet. Instead I got this. Hey, you ever rode a GTR?"

"No, heard it was fast."

Ken threw Cisco the keys. "Come on, let's go for a spin."

As they drove off, Ken texted Peter, "Be outside. I'm coming by. Remember what I told you."

Peter texted back, "Copy."

Cisco was enjoying the power of the twin turbo engines, swiftly switching the gears using the shift levels by the steering wheel. "Yea, bro, this shit is fast."

"It's them twin turbos. Hey, make a right. My boy just texted me. There he goes. Stop right here."

Peter went over to the car. "Hey, I need some more shit. We running low."

"Wow, shit moving fast. Okay, stop by the store. Talk to you later."

"Cool, see you in a few, Johnny."

Ken told Cisco, "Let's go back to the store."

When they got to the store, Cisco asked, "Hey, I don't mean to be in your business, but what is it you moving?"

"Come on, I'm going to show you better than I could tell you." Cisco followed Ken into the clothes' store. They went to the back and Ken showed him a brick of cocaine.

Cisco looked at it. "This shit is good? Do it come back?"

"Of course, and the numbers are nice."

Cisco grabbed it. "Oh yea, what number?"

"Three two and it's my last one. I'm waiting on my connect to bring me more."

"I get better numbers. But I'm on hold I should be straight soon. I got a big shipment coming in any day now."

Ken told him, "Well then, grab a few for me as long as the numbers are good."

"For sure, one hand washes another. Let me go get you that bread I got that sold right now."

"Okay." Cisco left the store. Ken turned off a video camera that recorded the whole conversation. He then called his superior Jeff Franconia, "Hey, boss, how you doing. I need a tail on somebody. Yea, twenty-four hours a day. And there's a big shipment coming any day now."

Over at the DEA office, his superior told him, "Keep up the good work."

YEMEN

Abdul arrived in Yemen. After saying good bye to Amreen and Jamil he met with his cousin Arif who took him to a house in Dhamar. They went into a backroom where his uncle Marudeen Khalil was wearing a gas mask, mixing chemicals in a plastic bowel.

Marudeen told him, "Finally, you are here. The thousands of miles you have traveled shows your commitment to our cause."

"I'm glad to be here. It is an honor. What is all this?" He was pointing to various plastic bowels full of a powdery substance.

Marudeen explained, "This is digoxin. It is extracted from a foxglove plant. Will kill a person if digested. And this here is ethylene glycol. It's used in a car's antifreeze. It knocks out organ systems. Over there, we have sodium cyanide that stops cells from using oxygen. A small dose of that could paralyze a full-grown camel. Here we have tabun, this causes convulsions and paralysis. There's some more stuff here, but I don't want to teach you too much at once. Your brain might short circuit. The plan is to spike up all the drugs you could get your hands on and start killing Americans by the mass."

Abdul asked, "Have you tested it, how does this work?"

Arif told him, "Yes, we have on a female. Now we just made it stronger. You will see with your own eyes." They mixed up a small quantity of the venomous powder with a little heroine. Then they jumped on camels and rode into the city. They found a bum who was an addict and took him to the mountains to offer him some of the spiked drugs. The addict sniffed the drugs. After a short time, he started to bleed from his mouth, eyes, nose, and ears. Then he gagged, falling to the floor and covering his face. Abdul could see something moving in the bum's pants. The spiked drugs that the addict consumed caused his bodily organs to slowly be pushed out his rectum. First, his intestines then his lungs and lastly, his heart that was still beating. The bum bled out and died.

Marudeen grabbed the addict's heart that was still pulsating and squeezed it as more blood was pouring out its valves. He looked at Abdul and said, "You see what it does!" He went over to his camel and fed it the heart.

Abdul threw up and wiped his mouth. "Wow, it's a gruesome but brilliant plan."

"The Americans love to *consume* drugs."

Marudeen told Abdul, "And not only will addicts die but also the ones that do it behind closed doors. Now we must show you how to make it so you could go back to the States and carry out your mission."

Abdul asked, "Yea, but just one thing, how do we get the drugs they are expensive? Where are we going to get the money from?"

Arif put his arms around Abdul. "Our brothers and sisters are waiting for you to get back to the States. They will help you carry out a mission that will provide you with all the money you need to buy tons of drugs." Both men started laughing over the body of the dead bum.

George Washington Bridge, New Jersey

Walter and his wife got off the Jersey's turnpike and drove into Fort Lee, New Jersey They dropped off Julio at a house where Juan Carlos was there waiting for him. Inside, Julio hugged his boss and asked him how was his trip.

"G5 is the best way to fly, out of sight out of mind." "Hey Julio let's play a game of pool you know I use to beat your ass all the time." "Things change boss I've been praticing." They head to the back of the house and Jaun Carlos flips a coin. "Heads or tail?" Julio said, "Heads." The coin lands on the pool table and it was tail. Jaun Carlos laughs. "You loose rack the balls. Hey how is Victor? After Julio racked the balls he went to the wall rack and grabbed a pool stick." He doing good. He should be getting back from a trip.

Victor was sniffing a bag of cocaine as he was waiting to pay the George Washington Bridge. He needed to wake up after that long trip up the East Coast. He looks around to see if anybody sees him and opens another bag.

Cisco left his house and drove off in his Corvette. He picked up Will and got on the highway. There was an undercover marked car following them. Victor stopped at a gas station and met up with Cisco and Will. Victor unloaded a caddy truck, and Cisco put a temporary plate on it and drove off.

Ken was in an unmarked car, taking pictures of them. He radioed to Agent Romo to follow Cisco who got followed to a house in a nice Yonkers neighborhood.

Will drove over the George Washington Bridge and got off in Fort Lee, leading Ken to the stash house where the rest of the gang was. Will knocked on the door and Sapo let him in. They hugged.

Sapo told Will, "Long time don't see."

"Yea, I know. Wow, you gained weight. That's the good life."

"Is them platanos."

Will hugged Juan Carlos. "How you been, did you get taller?"

"Yup, life goes fast."

Sapo brought out a bottle of whiskey. "Come on, let's drink to success and getting money."

Ken was outside taking pictures of the house and everybody that went in and out. The next day, Ken called Cisco to meet up at a motorcycle meet. There, Cisco told Will that Ken was on his way.

Will asked Cisco, "Dogs, you really trust him like that? You hardly know him."

"He good money. I did my homework on him. Shit, he even sold me some good ass coke."

"Make sure because there's a lot of rodents running the streets. Don't get lost. There's another large shipment on its way."

Ken arrives in his BMW motorcycle. He greeted Cisco and Will. A female called Will. He went over to her and gave her a kiss. She passed him a Corona and they started talking. Ken started to clean his bike with a cloth and discreetly pressed a button by the headlights, and a camera turned on. He then asked Cisco that his connection was dry, and he needed at least ten keys.

Cisco called Will over and asked him for ten keys and Will said, "Got you."

The next day, Cisco dropped the keys off at Ken's store. He had 320 thousand in a bag for Cisco as everything was being recorded. Ken said he needed more but to see if he could get a better number. Cisco said he had to talk to his boss and got on the phone. When he got off the phone, he said that Will was going to ask the boss who was in town from DR. Ken asked Cisco if he could handle big orders because he has some people coming in from out of town. Cisco told Ken that Will had mentioned there was another shipment coming in any day.

Manhattan,
New York City

Julio and Juan Carlos were at the Kawasaki dealer, buying two custom Campagna V-13 R T-REX 3 wheelers with the suicide doors, value at sixty thousand a piece. Across the street, there were two undercover agents snapping pictures. Julio took pictures of his brand new three wheeler in front of the dealer.

"I'm sending these flicks to Instagram." Juan Carlos snatched the phone from Julio and threw it on the street. A truck drove by and smashed it to pieces.

Julio asked him, "What happened, why you did that?"

"Dummy, don't you know that the feds are all over that shit. What's that, the i5? Don't worry, I'll get you the i6. See I just upgraded you. Come on, let's go see Kareem the jeweler."

They drove off in the T-REXs and got on the highway. They started racing each other, speeding at 140 miles an hour. In a blink of an eye, the undercover agents lost sight of them.

Agent Ramsey told his partner, "Shit, I got to bust one of them and confer state those bikes."

Julio and Juan Carlos were cruising through the diamond district in downtown Manhattan. Tourists took pictures of them, like they were celebrities. They parked in front of a jewelry store and two white females with large breasts asked Juan Carlos if they could take a picture in front of his T-REX.

He said, "Sure, if I could get your number."

One of the females replied, "Of course, where you from?"

Julio told them, "He's from Dominican Republic. Ever been there?"

"No, but I would love to go."

Juan Carlos whispered to Julio, "wow I wonder how many bricks fit in them big hooters." They both started to laugh. After taking a few pictures and exchanging numbers, the men entered the jewelry store and was greeted by Kareem, an Arab jeweler.

He told them, "Hey guys how you doing."

Julio shook Kareem's hand and so did Juan Carlos. Kareem told them, "My friends, come, come follow me."

They went to the back of the store, and Kareem showed them a block of twenty-four-carat gold. It was sitting on top of a floor scale. Juan Carlos went over to see how much the scale read, one hundred pounds.

Juan Carlos asked, "What's the market on twenty-four carats?"

Kareem said, "thirty-five dollars and twelve cents."

Jaun Carlos pulled out a calculator and started calculating. "Thirty five dollars and twelve cents a gram, times that by twenty eight, is nine hundred eighty-three dollors and thirty-six cents an once. Now times that by sixteen and you get fith teen thousand seven hundred thirty-three dollors and seventy six cents a pound. Times that by one hundred and that equals to one point five million seven hundred thirty-three dollors with seventy- six cents.

Jaun Carlos called Sapo and told him to bring one point five million seven hundred thirty three thousand. He turned to Kareem and said, "I need at least fifty more blocks of gold."

New Jersey

Goldo drove by a store that was having an art show. He saw a man on the sidewalk selling tin metal sculptures. He asked him, "Hey, this stuff looks pretty impressive. Why don't you have them on display inside?"

The artist told him, "They want a lot of money just to rent a space in there. Out here, I don't pay nothing."

Goldo laughed. "It don't look like you selling too much out here. Hey, I tell you what, could you sculpture animals?"

"I could make a sculpture out of you."

"Well I ain't trying for you to make an elephant. I like your work. I want to hire you to make a few pieces for me. My name is G."

"My name is Angelo, and sure, why not, as long as I'm paid for my time."

Juan Carlos and his gang unloaded the gold at a warehouse in New Jersey. Goldo showed up with Angelo. There was a few armed men inside with automatic weapons. He told Juan Carlos, "Hey, boss, I found a sculptor."

Angelo shook Juan Carlos's hand. "Pleasure to meet you. My name is Angelo."

"Okay, Angelo, are you ready to go to work and melt this gold down into animals?"

"Gold, why do you want to waste gold on silly animals, Mr. Juan Carlos?"

"That's really none of your business."

Goldo told Angelo, "I told you no questions, or they going to sculpt you into a wooden box."

Angelo looked at a guard who came over to him with a submachine gun then looked at the block of gold. "Okay, just write me a list of the animals you want sculpted."

Juan Carlos did the list consisting of various types of animals then left Angelo working and went to the other room to play cards. Juan Carlos started to talk to Julio and Goldo as he lit up a Cuban cigar, "The DEA only can catch you when other people start snitching. It's their strength. If there was no rats in the world, the DEA would be out of business. It's a rat-infested world, Julio."

Julio shuffled the cards, took a sip from his Corona, and recited a short rhyme that went "Yea, these filthy rodents, love to decapitate their heads and rolling, into the Fed building like I was bowling."

Carlos laughed. "Hey, that's a nice hook for a rap song." Then he threw in a hook. "Feds on me back for killing all these rats."

Goldo joined in on the hook, rhyming in Spanish, "Si mata, mata, mata to la ratas." They all broke out laughing. Angelo came in the room and showed them a replica of a rat he just finished molding. Goldo took it from his hand.

Juan Carlos told Goldo, "Let me see that." Goldo gave the gold rat to him. Juan Carlos got mad and threw it at Angelo, hitting him in the shoulder. He screamed at Angelo, "I fucking hate rats!"

Goldo told Angelo, "That was definitely not on the list. Just work with the list, papi."

The next day, the gang was at the New Jersey stash house. Goldo was sleeping, snoring on the couch. Juan Carlos woke Goldo up with a pot of cold water.

Goldo fell from the couch, mumbling, "What the fuck!"

"You snoring bastard get up. All you do is eat, blow up the bathroom, snore, and sleep."

Julio laughed. "Word up, bitches must hate your fat ass."

Goldo got back on the couch. "Na, 'cus I ain't cheap."

Julio said, laughing, "Shit, with that cheesy little dick, you got to pay like you weigh."

Juan Carlos told Goldo and Julio, "Stop clowning around. You see what time it is. You have to be at the airport by four to pick up the girls."

As they left the house, Ken was posing as a mailman in a mail truck half a block away. He was snapping pictures of the gang as they got in a van and left. Ken followed the drug traffickers to the airport and watched as ten females got into the van. Ken followed the van back to the house. He got on his phone and called for backup.

Inside the house, the girls were undressing, and a surgeon started procedures to perform surgery on the females to remove the cocaine from their breasts. By that time, Commander Franconia and his DEA agents were coordinating the raid around the corner. Ken told them there was at least ten females in the house along with five gang members. Then they all went back and surrounded the house.

Will was in a room where they had three naked females lying unconscious. He went over to one of them and lifted up the bedsheet to look up her legs. Ken, wearing a ski mask, with twenty agents broke down the door to the stash house and stormed in shouting, "This is the DEA, everybody freeze, get on the floor!"

Raul was behind a bar and shot at the agents as they were entering the house, injuring two of the them. Agents started shooting back. Julio was in a backroom and came out shooting a machine gun at the agents. Juan Carlos was in another room when he heard the gunshots. He came out with a Mac-10 and was also firing at agents. Sapo was in the kitchen, hiding by a refrigerator and shooting a pump shotgun that killed a DEA agent who passed by the kitchen entrance. Ken was behind the agent and let off a few rounds from his machine gun, killing Sapo.

Then Ken went in another room where there was naked woman running around scared. Agents were ordering them to get on the floor. From the outside of the house, neighbors were looking in shock as the windows from the stash house were getting shot out and lighting up from the gunfire. Will was trying to open a sliding glass door in the back of the house, attempting to escape. Ken came in and shot him in the ass and legs. He tried to grab a gun on a table. Ken shot him on the hand, but Will kept moving, so he shot him again in the back of his head. He then proceeded to clear rooms one by one with other agents. As he was cautiously entering one of the rooms, he saw Julio who quickly grabbed a female that was on the operation table, scared under a sheet. He used her as a shield as he was shooting at Ken and the other agents. Agent Romo returned fired, hitting the female and striking her in the chest, bursting the bags of cocaine in her filling the air with powder. Juan Carlos was behind an operating table and slid into another room with Julio who was following behind. They ran into a bathroom. Julio pushed in a dishwashing soap handle into the wall, and the whole tub rose up. The two men escaped by going down a staircase into a tunnel that led to another house a few hundred feet away. By the time the air cleared, Ken and the other agents were baffled because they couldn't find where Julio and Juan Carlos went. In the gun battle, two agents were critically injured and one died. As for the drug gang, three criminals died in the shoot out, and two female mules died while two others were hospitalized with none life-threatening injuries. The next day Ken went back to the stash house. He started to snoop around the bathroom and leaned on the soap dish. When he heard the noise of the bathtub starting to rise, he turned around quickly with his weapon drawn. He took out his flash light and went down into the tunnel. "So this is how they got away," he told himself.

Washington DC

Protecting the American people from terrorist threats was the reason the Department of Home Land Security (DHS) was created and remains their highest priority. Their vision is to secure a resilient nation that effectively prevents terrorism in ways that preserves freedom and prosperity.

The head of Home Land Security Ted Morgan was having a meeting with his staff. There were worries about a terrorist attack on US soil. They have a few extremist on their radar. On top of their list was Abdullah Salamah's, the leader of a radical extremist group from Yemen and a known master of explosives. Morgan went on to tell his staff, "He is responsible for the 1995 bombing of an American embassy that killed eighty Americans. Eventually, we had to evacuate because intelligence on the ground concluded it to be a dangerous and an unsafe place to have American personnel there."

There was a wanted photo of Abdullah Salamah's face with a five-million-dollar reward on his head. "Also on top of the list is the world order rebel leader Tabeeb Muhammad. We do know that at one point, he had united with Mabad Aik Saad, the leader of a Middle East terrorist group who has franchise in Pakistan, the Arabian Peninsula, and North Africa. However, Tabeeb Muhammad, who is a ruthless battlefield tactician that analysts suggest make his organization more attractive to young jihadists than that of Mabad Aik Saad, who is more an Islamic theologian. In any event, in October 2011, the US put a bounty on Tabeeb's head for ten million dollars, leading to his capture or death. What little intel we have of him is minimum expect for a few facts. Tabeeb is believed to have been born in Samarrai, north of Baghdad in 1971. A militant jihadist who was radicalized during the four years, he was held at Camp Buccua, a US facility in Southern Iraq where many rebel commanders were detained. This is where he emerged as the leader of a terrorist group that has become the enemy of many nations. He has never sworn allegiance to Mabad Aki Saad, the leader and mentor of a ruthless terror organization. Tabeeb Muhammad holds higher prestige among many Islamist militants. The way he operates is quite simple. Tabeeb has two deputies, one is responsible for overseeing the daily operations in Syria, and his other deputy oversees Iraq. Then there is the leadership council. Mr. Muhammad relies on a number of advisers with direct access to him and members of his council to help him handle religious differences, order executions, and ensure that policies conform to the terror group's doctrine. Then there is the cabinet. Managers oversee departments like finance, security, media, prisoners, and recruitments. Lastly, the local leaders, at least a dozen deputies across Iraq and Syria report to the deputy of each country. Evidence shows that many of their high-ranking military officers come from the forces of the once dictator Saddam Hussein. One of their key recruiting strategies via social media is sending out ninety thousand messages a day. There is going to be a briefing at the White House later on today on foreign policy."

Manhattan,
New York City

Ken was at the DEA office getting ready to go over the gang's activities with Commander Franconia and other agents. Ken turned to the agents in the room. "Okay, everybody, grab a seat so we could go over the activities of the Colombian cartel, the Bandidos and their associates Los El Hermano Fuertes who have been flooding the East Coast with drugs for the last decade." Ken handed out pictures of the gang to the agents in the room. He started to brief them, "Okay, this is what we got so far. After the raid in the Jersey stash house, we arrested a group of Dominican women with fake passports. Aside from entering the country illegally, they were also charged with trafficking and other narcotic violations. Well now, we are fortunate to have one of the female mules Juanita Cruz cooperating fully with this ongoing investigation. According to a written statement when we interviewed her, she said the leader of the drug gang of the Hermano Fuertes was repeatedly heard being called Juan Carlos. Very little is known of him except that he cold-bloodedly shot and killed a potential female smuggler named Desiree Cruz, the sister of Juanita Cruz. In her testimony, she also stated her younger sister died because she refused, not wanting to have keys of cocaine sewed into her breast to transport the drugs back to the States. So Juan Carlos killed her to instill fear in the rest of the women who had no choice but to carry out his trafficking operation. He also promised them that their families were going to be killed if they did not cooperate. We sent pictures of him to our DEA affiliates in Santo Domingo and are waiting to see if he pops up in their criminal database. Based on Miss Cruz's testimony, we were able to obtain an arrest warrant for Juan Carlos. Juanita Cruz also claims that he was in the house when it got raided. I got a slight glimpse of him but couldn't get a clear shot because it looked like it was snowing in there with all that powder in the air. He got away along with another Spanish male whose name is Julio Mendez a top lieutenant for the gang. We believe he is the one responsible for the attempted murder of two of our agents, Jessica Riley and Agent Muller back in January who are still in the hospital fighting for their lives. And if you sadly remember, K-9 Sammy was shot and killed in that same raid. Slowly but surely, we are disrupting and dismantling this violent organization. The raid in the Jersey stash house which resulted in a bloody shootout and ended in us killing three of their top lieutenants Gejelmo Ortiz a.k.a. Sapo, Raul Delgado, and Will Santiago."

Franconia intervenes, yelling, "And we're going to keep killing those cockroaches!"

Ken continued, "Also on our list is Devon Daniels a.k.a. Cisco, another top lieutenant who is involved heavily with the crews day-to-day drug activities. In tailing Cisco, it paid off tremendously. He led us to Will Santiago who led us to the gangs stash house which ultimately disrupted their operation confer stating a whole cache of weapons and drugs. In addition, we were able to detain and flip that female drug mule Juanita Cruz who I mentioned earlier. Basically, with her testimony, we will be able to execute secret indictments through a Federal Grand Jury on these individuals. The investigation originally started when Devon Daniels a.k.a. Cisco purchased a key of cocaine from me."

Franconia yelled, "That was slick police work. Sometimes, you got to get down and dirty on them."

Ken continued, "It was part of a counter operation called Wheel 'Em In. Gaining his confidence that led to a large transaction in which on March 10, he sold ten keys of cocaine to a federal agent."

Ken raised his fingers as to indicate it was him that Cisco made that sale to. "We decided to leave him on the streets so he could lead us to the rest of the gang. Last on our list, but surely not forgotten, who back on February 6 we placed a tail on. Another interesting character that Cisco, who was so kind of him to also lead us to whom we believe is the gang's driver, Victor Alvarez. Here, he is shown with Cisco at a gas station in the Washington Heights section on April third, delivering an SUV that a team of undercover federal agents placed under surveillance and tailed it to the gang's stash house, recording them unloading several kilos of cocaine. It is our belief that the gang is using the tractor trailer to haul tons of cocaine up and down the East Coast. This is a well-connected, highly skilled organization that has close ties with the leader of the Colombian cartel, the Bandidos."

Commander Franconia got up from his seat. "We are working with our international resources, but these individuals for years have been elusive and untouchable, very well connected in Colombia with political ties. They are known to contribute heavily to political causes for their benefits, corrupt politicians, and rig elections."

One of the agents said out loud, "So these thugs have the country in their pockets."

Ken replied, "Sure looks like it."

All the DEA agents were staring at a picture of Jose Luis Rios sitting in a yellow Lamborghini Veneno Roadster with a monkey sitting on his lap and a cheetah sitting on the passenger seat.

QUEENS, NEW YORK

Abdul was aboard a commercial jet, looking out the window. As the jetliner was descending from the clouds, New York City emerged and all the bright lights became visible. Abdul told himself, "Finally, I'm back. America, brace yourself." His cousins Mohammed, Nazar and Zyan picked him up at the airport. They hugged one another, got in the car, and drove off.

Nazar asked Abdul, "Welcome back. How was your trip?"

"Everything went well. Our brothers over there send you their love and are praying for us."

Mohammed drove on the Brooklyn, Queens expressway. Abdul asked, "How is everybody doing?"

Zyan grabbed his hand. "We all are fine, just waiting for you. Did you accomplish what you set out to do in Yemen?"

"Everything is going according to plan. Soon the people of America are going to be in for a big surprise."

"Good, we can't wait to contribute in every way possible."

Mohammed agreed, "Yes, we all are anxious to participate."

Mohammed got off the highway and passed the Barclays Center.

Zyan told Abdul, "You must be hungry?"

Abdul yawns. "I could eat a camel."

Ken was driving on the FDR. He got off the twenty-third exit and drove up to the Bellevue Hospital where his sister was in a coma, fighting for her life for the last three months. He entered her room with some flowers. Their cousin Jasmine was sitting in the room, sleeping on a chair. She woke up when she heard the door open.

"Johnny." She stood up and hugged her cousin.

Ken asked her, "How long you been here?"

"Since the morning. I promised your mother that I will watch over her so she could go home and rest."

"Thanks." He went over to his sister's bed and grabbed her hand. He closed his eyes and prayed, "Lord, please give her the strength she needs to wake up. She don't deserve this."

Jasmine joined in the prayer, "God, please let her wake up. I really miss her." Jasmine started to cry.

Ken hugged her. "She is going to pull through. We just got to keep praying." He left the room. Ken's eyes started to tear up as he passed by a nurse who asked him, "Is everything okay, sir?"

Ken shook his head. "No, it's not." He got in his car and drove off, getting on the highway. He started to increase the speed of his Nissan, thinking about the shootout he had in the Jersey raid. He screamed, "I wish I would've got 'em!" Ken pulled up into his mother's driveway.

She was on the porch, sitting on a rocking chair. Ken exited the car carrying some flowers. He walked up to his mother and gave her a kiss. "Mom, how are you?"

"Not too well. I'm ready to head out to see how Jessica is doing. Jasmine's been there all day."

"Where is Dad?"

"He is inside changing." Ken went in the house and entered his father's room. "Dad." He saw his father sitting on the bed, looking at a picture of Jessica holding and patting her little Yorkie.

He told Ken, "Lulu misses Jessica. Every time somebody comes through the door, she thinks it's her." Ken grabbed Lulu and gave her a kiss, "Don't worry, Lulu, Jessica will be home soon."

DELAWARE

It was 9:00 a.m. Abdul was in the back of a van on his way to rob the West Delaware Bank located in the downtown Delaware area. It was the beginning of a larger mission he needed to do so he could obtain the cash to purchase large shipments of cocaine so he could contaminate the drugs. He knew America was into substance abuse and was going to take full advantage of that. His deadly plan was to kill millions of American addicts along with the large population of social users. The van turned the corner and parked in front of the bank. He gripped his machine gun and cocked it back. He was with two of his cousins Mohammed and Rahan plus four other extremist women named Aasia, Cantara, Fellah, and Hazirah. They were there to assist Abdul to carry out the brazen heist in broad daylight.

The women were under the command of a high-ranking Yemen Military by the name of Abe-El-Kader Wahib, who was an affiliate with a Middle East terrorist network. The females were a mixture of Australian, French, and US nationalities, ranging from seventeen to twenty-five years old. They were part of an alarmingly growing trend of young women who were radicalized and brainwashed through social media.

They were planning to leave to Syria and join other militant women in the war against other radical groups that chose to resist their cause. But first, the women were ordered to help Abdul, one of the many lone wolves in America who were raising funds that later would be used to launch a chemical attack on US soil. In Arabic, Abdul radioed to his other two cousins Zyan and Nasar who were one block away in a park, feeding pigeons.

"Everybody in position?"

Zyan answered in Arabic, "Yes, we are. All is as planned."

Before entering the bank, Mohammad said a short Arabic prayer. Then all six of his accomplices stormed the bank with their automatic weapons drawn. Abdul and the terrorist women robbing the bank were dressed in full-length black burkas, and their faces were covered in a veil that all could be seen were their treacherous eyes.

Once in the bank, Abdul shot an armed guard to death then fired his weapon into the ceiling, screaming, "Everybody on the floor. Do as you are told, and you will not be harmed!" Customers and bank employees were scrambling to get on the floor. Mary Jane Taylor, the manager of the bank, was sitting behind her desk when the bandits stormed in. Before she got on the ground, she pressed a button under her desk, alerting the authorities. Cantara and Fellah ordered the customers to get up and head toward the back of the bank. Hazirah started to clean out the tellers stations, taking large packs of money and placing them in a duffel bag. Abdul forced the manager to the back. He told her, "If you do not open the safe, I will blow your head off and kill everyone here, do you understand?"

Mary Jane nodded yes. "Okay, okay, just don't hurt me."

The silent alarm that went off alerted the police who were on their way. Officer Leonard was in his patrol car, watching his overweight partner Kevin Reynolds walk out of a coffee shop toward him. When Watkins got the call on his radio, Watkins told Reynolds, "Hurry up, man! Drop them donuts. The Delaware Bank is getting robbed!"

"No shit, I'm still taking my donuts with me." Two other units that were in the vicinity started to head toward the bank. Over at the bank, Aasia stood watching the front entrance while the rest of the bandits emptied out the vault. They forced everybody except Mary Jane into the walk-in safe and locked the door. "What about me?" said the manager.

Cantara told her, "We might need you."

"Please don't kill me," Mary Jane begged. She started to cry as she fell to the floor.

Abdul hit her with the edge of his gun on her head. "Bitch, get up and shut up!"

Officer Reynolds and his partner Watkins were the first on the scene. Everything seemed normal and quiet. Reynolds had his gun drawn as he slowly crept up to the front window of the bank. He took a peek inside and noticed a dead guard on the ground with a pool of blood surrounding his body. Reynolds partner Watkins was walking behind him, positioning himself by the side of the bank door.

When Abdul saw Officer Reynolds, he immediately let off a round out of his machine gun. A barrage of bullets shattered the front bank window, striking Reynolds in the arm, neck, and face. He dropped to the ground as blood was leaking out his neck from a bullet that penetrated his jugular vein.

Watkins screamed, "No, Kev!" Leonard attempted to go over to his dying partner but was stopped by a hail of bullets from Abdul's machine gun. Two other police units arrived and positioned themselves in the back of their police cars across the street from the bank. One officer opened the trunk of his patrol car and pulled out a shotgun and an assault rifle, which he passed to his partner. The bank robbers started to fire their weapons toward the officers who just arrived. As the cops returned fire, bullets were hitting the counters and light fixtures in the bank, making the robbers duck for cover. The Delaware Police Department had dispatched a SWAT team who were a few minutes away. Cantara radioed in to Abdul's cousins Zyan and Nasar who were one block away, sitting in a park and holding remote controls with six-inch monitors. Two small drones with cameras and mini mac machine guns mounted to their frames flew up in the air and headed toward the bank.

Cantara was heard saying through the radio, "We trapped. Get us out of here!"

"On our way," Zyan screamed through the walkie-talkie.

Two more patrol cars arrived at the scene. The bandits started to fire their weapons at them. Officers returned fire. But then out of the sky from behind them, two drones surprisingly hovered over the officers and open fired, killing all of the them except Watkins who was injured but managed to fire his weapon and shoot down one of the drones. He got up and started to run down the street as the second drone was behind him, shooting in his path. People were running into shops and ducking behind parked cars. Zyan was controlling the second drone from a truck driven by Nasar who was racing toward the bank. Zyan was watching from the screen on his remote control, laughing. "Got you now, piggy!"

Watkins ran out of bullets and fell to the ground as the drone hovered over him. He saw the gun barrel that was attached to the drone and screamed, "No!"

Zyan pressed the shoot button on his remote control panel, and the drone shot Watkins to death. Nasar and Zyan drove the truck on the sidewalk and stopped in front of the bank. The SWAT team arrived and set up position across the street from the bank. Nasar radioed to Abdul, "We are surrounded by pigs. They are all over the place!"

Abdul radioed back, "Okay we are putting plan B in motion. We are taking the hostages!" Abdul ordered Hazirah and Fellah to go and get the hostages who were locked in the vault. Cantara grabbed the manager and headed toward the back. Once there, she ordered Mary Jane to open the safe. Cantara told her, "See, aren't you glad we didn't lock you in the safe."

The bank's phone rang. Abdul answered it, "This is the Delaware Bank, how may I help you?"

Outside across the street from the bank, Sergeant Dan Tompskin was standing next to Police Officer Tim Wordy, a hostage negotiator who was on the phone with Abdul.

"This is Officer Tim Wordy, is everybody okay there?"

Abdul laughed "Yea, for the moment, everybody's still alive. We are just making a withdrawal."

Wordy responded, "What are your demands? Are you the one in charge there?"

"Listen here, you see those dead officers your corners are scraping off the ground all around you. Well, we have no quarrels of killing all the hostages including ourselves if our demands are not met or respected. Now you see that truck in front of you? We are all coming out and are leaving in it. If you try to stop us, we will detonate a bomb and everybody here including yourselves are going up in smoke. Is that understood?"

"Let the hostages go and you're free to leave. That's the best I could do."

Abdul replied, screaming, "That's the best you could do! I'm going to show you that you could do better!" Abdul told Cantara to dress up the manager in one of the full-length black burkas with a veil covering her face. Cantara rummaged into a duffel bag and pulled out the black burkas.

Mary Jane asked, "But why do you want me to put that on for?"

Cantara screamed, "Just do what you're told or face death!"

Abdul came from behind and ripped her dress off. She stood standing there in her bra and panties. Eventually, she had no choice but to change. Abdul then strapped a bomb, consisting of four dynamite sticks that were connected to a detonator on the top of her head. She broke out in tears and said, "Please, I'm a mother of two kids. Don't do this to me. I don't want to die."

Abdul told her, "Don't worry. I won't make you suffer."

She cried on sadly. "But you are." Abdul proceeded to wrap a thin wire under her chin and around her neck to secure the bomb in place as all the frightened hostages watched in horror.

He told her, "You're free to go" and walked her to the front door. He kicked her in the ass and told her, "Run, bitch!"

Mary Jane ran out the bank screaming, "Help me, help me!" She ran across the street, heading toward the police officers who were taking cover.

One officer screamed, "She has a bomb!"

Another officer open fired then all the officers started to shoot toward the charging bank manager, killing her instantly. She dropped to the ground and then the bomb went off, blowing her up and windows from cars and buildings in the surrounding area.

The phone in the bank rang again. Abdul picked it up. "This is the Delaware Bank. I'm afraid the manager can no longer help you because you were not in compliance with the rules. And now she is dead in the middle of the street from friendly gunfire and a head bomb."

Tim told his sergeant, "Sir, we are dealing with a psycho."

Abdul ordered Hazirah to dress up all the hostages with the burkas. "Okay, I'm on it."

The sergeant told Tim, "Let them all leave."

Tim related the message. "Okay, have it your way."

Abdul laughed and said, "Of course, is my way or the highway and that's exactly where we're going. One more thing, officer, if you attempt to follow us, I will start shooting hostages and throw 'em out the back of the truck onto the highway. So if you don't want to be scraping up road kill, I suggest you stay away. The bank is now closed until further notice."

The sergeant told one of his officers to call for a chopper.

Abdul radioed to Zyan, "We're coming out."

Zyan replied, "Copy."

Zyan lifted up the back door to the truck as Nasar was maneuvering the drone, making it face toward the police officers across the street.

The sergeant told Tim, "Wow, we got to get some of those."

Inside the bank, Haziarh hid her weapon under her burkas and walked out the bank in the middle of four hostages who were carrying the duffel bags of money. The hostages helped put the money bags in the truck. Cantara walked out in between another four hostages. Then Aasia walked out the same way between four more hostages. Lastly, Abdul and Fellah came out with the rest of the hostages. Once in the truck, Abdul told Nasar to drive off. Zyan said, "You hear that helicopter?"

Abdul looked at the hostages and asked them, "Who knows how to drive?" Nobody said anything.

Cantara cocked her weapon back, screaming, "Perhaps I should start shooting them one by one until somebody says they know how to drive!"

Everybody put their hands up. The hostages started saying, "I know, I could drive, I got a permit!"

Nazar was looking at the screen of his remote panel. He navigated the drone toward the officers vehicles and shot out the tires. Officers returned fire but missed the drone as it flew high in the air. Tim was with the sergeant in an unmarked car, following the truck as it got on the highway. Zyan got on the highway and noticed an unmarked car following them through his side view mirror, a few cars behind. Nasar radioed to Abdul and told him, "There is a cop car following us."

Abdul opened the back door of the truck and grabbed a hostage. He punched the nervous man in the throat with a sharp item, creating a hole in his Adam's apple and causing blood to gush out. Abdul then pushed the frightened man out of the truck, and Cantara shot the hostage in the back as he rolled on the highway's pavement. The cars that were behind the truck tried to avoid running over the dead man, but it was impossible. The dead body got ran over by three different cars, which created a series of crashes with other cars that were behind them on the highway.

Nazar navigated the drone and pointed the machine guns at the sergeant's patrol car and fired off a round that penetrated through the windshield of officer Wordy's patrol car, striking him in the neck. Blood started to gush all over the windshield. The sergeant was trying to steer the car from crashing, but it crashed into a pole, killing both officers instantly. Zyan got off the highway. He looked up and saw the helicopter that had been following them from the bank. He drove into a five-story building parking lot. The helicopter was radioing to other police officers that the truck went into a parking lot building on Weldon and Surmise Avenue.

A patrol car radioed to the central command, saying they were minutes away. Everybody except the hostages got out of the truck. The robbers unloaded the duffel bags and placed them in a white minivan. There were also two identical black mini vans stationed there in case plan B had to be executed. Abdul took out three hostages from the truck and told them if they wanted to live, they'd do as he said. They all agreed. He told one of the three hostages to get into the truck. He was instructed to exit the building and make a right onto the highway and not to stop, or everybody in the back of the truck was going to get blown up. The hostage agreed and drove the truck out the parking lot building. As he made a right on to the street, he crashed into a police car arriving on the scene. The officer's car lost control and crashed into a store front, injuring and killing dozens. The officer that was driving died as he exited the patrol car. His partner was radioing for help when the drone hovered upon him, saying, "I wouldn't do that if i was you." Then Nazar fired off a round, killing the officer.

Back in the parking lot building, Abdul told one of the two other hostages to get in one of the two black minivan that he pointed to and drive off. "When you exit, make a left." The hostage complied but was moving too slow, so Abdul kicked her in the back off her ass, screaming to her, "Hurry up, bitch." She got in the van, drove out of the parking lot, and blended into the traffic.

Then, Abdul put the remaining hostage in the other black minivan and told her to drive out the parking lot building in the opposite direction. The helicopter was radioing to other police officers that the truck hit a patrol car on Alden Street. The pilot in the chopper also said, "Two other black minivans had left the building in separate directions." The helicopter followed the truck. Meanwhile, another police chopper was dispatched to the vicinity to locate the black minivans. Abdul and his team waited for five minutes. The drone flew back into the parking lot.

Jokingly, Nazar said on his voice device, "Clear to leave." That came from the microphone speaker of his drone. Then they all left the parking lot in a white minivan. Police officers were scrambling, looking for the two black minivans. Delaware State Troopers tried to pull over the truck but the driver was afraid to stop because he thought the hostages in the back of the truck would be killed if he pulled over. Eventually, the Troopers put a spike strip up ahead on the highway. As the truck drove through it, the wheels ripped apart, causing the truck to flip over on its side, sliding until crashing into a utility pole and splitting the whole back cabin into two pieces. When the troopers got to the horrific crash scene, there were dead and critically injured bodies lying all over the highway, getting run over by other cars. As the second police chopper was hovering over one of the decoy minivans, cops stopped and searched it but did not find any of the bank robbers. The other mini van had stopped at a gas station and called the police who immediately arrived.

New Jersey

Juan Carlos was in a helicopter flying with a female companion over the George Washington Bridge. The chopper flew to a warehouse in New Jersey and landed by a bunch of commercial buildings. He and the blond exited the aircraft. As they were walking the short distance to the warehouse, she started complaining, "Damn these high heels making my feet hurt."

Juan Carlos looked at her feet. "First of all, them feet look too big for them shoes. And second of all, why you spend so much money for them, if they making your toes cry? Ya could be so dumb sometimes."

She looked at him with a smirk. "Really, you think you're real funny."

They got to the warehouse, and Juan Carlos knocked on the door. An armed man let them in. Juan Carlos asked, "Pito, how's everything coming along?"

"Everything is almost packed and ready to go, boss."

Juan Carlos went over to Angelo. "Nice work."

Angelo just finished sculpting a gold rooster. "I'm glad you like it, sir."

There was another armed man standing next to the rest of the gold sculptures. Also in the secluded warehouse by the water were other workers who were placing the twenty or more different types of twenty-four-carat gold sculptures and appliances into wooden crates. Angelo approached Juan Carlos and couldn't thank him enough for giving him the opportunity to work and for providing work for his brother Manuel who was also a sculpture which at that time was unemployed.

Juan Carlos replied, "As long you keep creating different sculptures, you will always have a job. I like your brothers idea how he molded the gold into a stove and a refrigerator." Manual was paint spraying a gold and silver microwave as Juan Carlos looked on eagerly.

Juan went outside and walked over to the helicopter. He took out a phone and called Colombia. "Amigo, como estas (how are you doing)?".

Jose Luis could be heard on the other line. "Juansito, how is everything?"

Juan Carlos walked over to the edge of the boardwalk by the water. "Good, hermanito (brother)."

"Hey Juan, a shipment of one ton of cocaine is en route. If everything goes well, it should be arriving tomorrow," he told him in Spanish.

Juan Carlos picked up a rock and threw into the water, trying to hit a seagull that flew away. "Okay good, and in about three days, you going to get a one-hundred-million-dollar surprise."

"Oh si (yes), okay, I call you when it arrives."

When Juan Carlos came back to the warehouse. Manual showed him a gold bedframe, chair, lamp, and a round mirror. "Wow, that's beautiful, my friend. Could you do a boat?"

MANHATTAN, NEW YORK CITY

Cisco and Julio were speeding on the West Side High in there motorcycles, weaving in and out of traffic. Officers in an unmarked car radioed to another unit at the end of the highway on 59th Street to pick up the tail. As the two bikes went past them, they continued to follow Cisco and Julio who were riding on just the back wheel along the West Side. They rode to Kareem's cousin's jewelry store and were looking at diamond watches. Julio tries on an eighteen-carat Rolex with a diamond bezel. He asked Cisco, "You like it?"

"Hell yea, let me try it on." Julio took off the watch and passed it to Cisco who put it on. He was looking in the mirror and asked the jeweler, "How much?"

Julio laughed. "Baby boy, if you got to ask, that mean you can't afford it."

The jeweler leaned closer to the guys. I can let the two of them go for forty a piece. And that's a good deal."

Julio shook his hand. "Let me get two of those." He started to pull out money from his knapsack.

Cisco put his arm around Julio. "Wow, bro, good looking. Only real niggas do that."

"Just keep watching my back and don't ever flip on me."

"You crazy. We go way back. You remember when we was small, and I did that burglary and came off and what did I get you, your first bike."

"Word up, it was an Apollo Silver five speed."

The DEA was watching them from a distance, snapping pictures as they left the store.

Julio puts his diamond watch in the sunlight. He shook his head up and down and told himself, "Nice."

The DEA agent who was watching them with binoculars got blinded from the shining of the high-quality diamonds. Julio and Cisco got on their motorcycles and left. Julio saw some females waiting for the light to change so they could cross the street. He popped a wheelie, showing off.

One of the females screamed, "Can I get a ride!"

Julio screamed back, "You too fat!"

When they stopped at the light, the females were crossing the street, and Cisco motioned to one of them to get on. She said, "What about my friend?"

Julio started to make his back wheel rotate as he was holding the front brake, making smoke come out the back wheel. Cisco told the girls to get on. One of the girls got on the back of Cisco's bike and her friend jumped on Julio's bike.

Julio told her, "You crazy?"

Cisco saw the cops and said, "Let's get out of here. The cops are coming!"

Julio did a wheelie that the chubby girl could not hold on, and she fell off the bike as Julio sped off. A patrol car saw Julio and Cisco doing stunts on their bikes. The cops told them on the car intercom to pull over. Cisco put up his middle finger at the cops as he and Julio fled the area. The cops started chasing them. The DEA agents that were following the drug dealers joined the chase and were mad that the cops were interfering with their investigation. Julio, Cisco, and the female got on the highway and disappeared, doing 150 miles an hour.

The agents caught up with the cops and told them, "Way to go. You just blew a tale we had on those suspects who we've been following for months.

The cop said, "Sorry, we didn't know. You should get a faster car."

Victor was in Starbucks having a cup of coffee. There was a pretty college student sitting opposite from him, eating a bagel and looking at her laptop. Victor started to fantasize walking over to her and kissing her on the mouth. When he opened his eyes, she was staring back at him, shaking her head in disgust. Victor got a text with an address. He got up and blew a kiss at the college student as he walked out the coffee shop. He got on the train on 68th Street in Lexington and headed uptown to Spanish Harlem. He exited the 125 and Park Avenue Station. He walked up two blocks to a parking lot and picked up his truck. He put on his GPS and started to follow the route. He made a call to his son, "Hey, what you up to, son?"

"Nothing much, just playing online. When you coming home, Dad? I'm hungry."

"There's food in the fridge. Get your lazy ass up and make something. And don't burn the house down." Victor headed toward New Jersey. He hung up the phone and turned on the radio. He drove a few more miles then the GPS said, "Your destination is on your right." He drove into a dock port where ships brought in containers from all over the world. He met with a dock inspector and handed him a large envelope of cash.

The inspector said, "Thank you for your contribution." He got on his walkie-talkie and told a worker to pull out container number 54595. He told Victor, "Just bring your truck around the back."

Victor shook his hand. "Okay, thank you very much." Victor got in his truck and drove around the back. A dock worker motioned him to park at the end of the loading dock. There Victor backed up his truck and the dock worker helped him connect the container to his truck. Victor gave him a tip and drove out of the docking area. He got on the highway and drove to a storage building where Juan Carlos's helpers were there to help unload the contents of the container. There were all sorts of furniture with bricks of cocaine concealed in them.

Abdul and his cousins came out the Gucci store carrying a lot of bags. Zyan asked, "Why did we have to spend so much money in that store? That was a waste of money. You know what I could have got in Marshall's for that type of bread."

Abdul told him, "Appearance is how people judge you. If they see you with a pair of pro-Keds, they look at you like you cheap. But if they see you in a pair of Gucci shoes, they think you balling. They respect you more. And where we going and the people we going to see, it is very important we look like ballers."

Rahan asked, "Then why we just didn't go to Models and get basketball uniforms?"

Abdul looked at him and shook his head. They got in a minivan and drove by Madison Square Garden. Then they got on the highway and on to the Brooklyn Queens expressway, heading toward Abdul's house to eat. Once they arrived, Abdul hugged his wife Hindah and two sons Aiman and Walil, who were happy to see him. Hindah told her husband the food was almost done. His kids were jumping up and down on the huge pile of money that was stolen from the Delaware bank. Abdul told his sons to go wash up and get ready for dinner as he and his cousins started to change. Abdul gave them a few gold chains to put on. He said they were fake.

Zyan grabbed one. "Wow, they look real."

Abdul handed him some designer shades. "Yea, like a lot of these rappers who be wearing fake jewelry. Just don't sweat too much. They might turn green and your cover might get blown." After the cousins changed, he told them, "Okay now, all of you look like drug dealers. The next phase of the operation is going down tonight."

Hindah came in the living room and told the guys, "Food is done, everybody." She screamed to Aiman and Wali to come out to eat. Everybody sat on the floor. In the middle of them was a large round steel bowl with rice, chopped chicken, and steamed vegetables. They all started to eat, grabbing the food with their fingers.

Abdul's son Aiman asked, "Why do we have to eat with our fingers?"

Abdul smiled. "Why do you think God gave you fingers for?"

Brooklyn, New York

Asma came home with her friend Avenda. She greeted Asma's father and mother. Then the girls went to Asma's room to catch up on some homework. Asma's parents Fariah and Farhan were in the living room watching TV. He told her, "Look how thousands of Muslims are being displaced, terrorized, and slaughtered."

The newscaster was elaborating on the current situation, "Nobody in Washington seemed to understand how this terror group is growing power at a disturbing rapid pace. It's all part of a bloody holy war between the Sunnis and Shites that's been going on for seven centuries. This new terrorist army is gaining ground, recruits, and military power. Because their leader has succeeded in portraying himself as the protector of Sunnis. That will prevent the Shites from taking over. His propaganda shows success against US and Saudi coalition air attacks who are allied with the Shites in Baghdad, the Al-ssad Alawite dynasty in Damascus, Hezbollah in Lebanon and the Ayalloh in Teran. That's why this terrorist cult continues to attract Sunni militants by the thousands from every part of the world including the US."

Farhan looked at his wife and shook his head in disbelief. The newscaster continues to say, "Over two hundred thousand Muslims have died in the last two years. The king of Jordan King Ahdullah is quoted as saying, 'This is a war inside Islam. A fight between good and evil.'"

Back in Asma's room, Avenda told Asma, "Yousef gave me a number to call. They are going to help me get to Syria."

"After all the bad things you are hearing, you still want to go and risk your life, not knowing what to expect."

"Well, why don't you come with me, and if it's not what it is, we can come back. Please don't let me go by myself. Together we could watch each other's back."

"Are you losing your mind? My mother and father will kill me."

"Not if they don't know."

Asma's brother Iman met with Zyan outside the mosque. "Iman, we are planning a trip to the Middle East. Are you going to come with us to Syria? We must join the war."

"Are you crazy? You want to abandon your family here to go and kill other Muslims. A real Muslim do not kill other Muslims. Don't you see they are brainwashing you. You're just going to die, and the revolution still continues."

"They are calling, and I can't just ignore their calls."

"Yea, they are calling because they want you to become a killing machine, and when the war is over, how much blood is going to be in your hands?"

"You don't get it. The cause is to defend and expand. You see the thousands of Muslims who are marching across the world to join. Why won't you do the same?"

"You foolish frog, because I am a real Muslim that represents God while you shame him and millions who are normal, decent, law-abiding citizens who are trying to raise their families on their beliefs and religion. Besides that, they will arrest you if you get caught leaving like they did that American girl from Colorado. The government gave her four years to deter others form following in her footsteps."

"I feel it is worth it for me to leave. I've been talking to Jaseena in Syria. She is out there waiting for me. She tells me Islam is under attack. She wants me to contribute to the building of a new society and establishment of the caliphate. My sister already left with two of her school friends. They told her it's their duty to migrate to the Islamic state, a sisterhood thing."

Iman started to laugh. "That's what she told you."

"Yes, my sister and her friends are going to become jihadi brides."

"I'm glad my sister is not brainwashed like yours is. Don't you know once you're there, they quickly marry you so you feel obligated to stay because you have a new family to raise. Maybe the real reason you want to go is because you feel like you're going on an adventure. Stay here and spare your life. Don't wind up blown up in some battlefield."

Manhattan, New York City

Julio and Cisco were at a club downtown hanging out in the VIP section drinking with a couple of blondes. Julio told Cisco, "I opened up the bike hard earlier today when we were getting chased."

"Yea, bro, that was fun getting on the highway and dusting them pigs. Too bad you gave that heifer a road rash."

Julio laughed. "Yea well, she should've hung on, besides the nerve of her jumping on my bike. You didn't see how she lifted my whole front up?" Julio looked at his watch. "This guy Ab is late. What a geek. You remember him when we was in elementary school. He was always wearing that scarf over his head."

Cisco laughed. "Yea, he used to stink too. Didn't believe in deodorant."

Julio leaned over to Cisco. "Yea well, now I hear he's doing big things, buying big things. Talk of the devil."

Abdul and his cousins plus a family friend were walking toward the VIP. He shook Julio's hand. "Long time, my friend."

Julio looked up at Abdul. "Wow, I see you lost the scarf."

"Times have changed."

Cisco gave him a hug and told him, "And you smell better now."

Abdul introduced his cousins to Julio and Cisco. They all sat down and Julio offered them drinks, but they declined. It was against their religion. So Cisco ordered the guys mineral water. Julio told the blondes to go on the dance floor with Abdul's cousins so he and Abdul could talk business. "So, Ab, what you been doing all these years?" Julio asked.

"How you Americans put it, I've been grinding. Then my parents died and left me and my brothers the family business, but we messed that up and bailed out. We sold it to another company that knew what they were doing. So now, I just need a good plug to keep my fortune growing and what better way, the American way, getting our hands on what's in demand, that cocania."

Cisco asked Abdul, "What, you thinking about buying?"

Abdul leaned toward him, "Three hundred keys, and as you Americans put it, what street you on?"

"Wow, three hundred keys, and you talking straight C.O.D.?"

"Yes, but can you deliver, or are you wasting my time?"

Julio asked, "Is thirty-two a good street for you?"

Abdul shook his head no. "I'm more like in the thirty-ish street."

Julio looked at Cisco then Abdul. "I could see you there."

Abdul asked, "Can I see you tomorrow?"

"I call you." The men shook hands.

Abdul gets up and leaves. He was looking for his cousins but did not see them. Julio got up.

"Damn, I got to take a shit." He looked at Cisco and told him, "It must be them nasty pork chops your girl cooked."

Julio was in the toilet taking a crap. He heard some Arabs talking in Arabic, saying, "What a brilliant plan Abdul is carrying out, buying all them drugs from them two clowns and poisoning the drugs to start killing all these American addicts."

They started laughing. Nasar asked in English, "How many addicts you think are going to die when we contaminate all them drugs?"

Abdul's cousin Rahan speculated. "Millions, I hope." Everybody left the bathroom, but their friend Wisam stood behind, combing his hair.

He told them, "I be right out."

Julio grabbed Wisam from behind and dragged him inside the stall, where he was taking a crap. He asked him, "What the hell were you talking about in Arabic?"

"Fuck you, mind your business!"

"Oh yea." Then he smashed his head inside the toilet. When he lifted Wisam back up, his face was full of crap, and Julio kept sticking his head in and out the toilet. Finally, Wisam told Julio what his friends were saying in Arabic. Then Julio snapped his neck, killing him. Wisam's chain fell off his neck onto the ground. Julio left him with his head inside the toilet and flushed it before he left the stall. Then he exited the bathroom.

Shortly afterward, a worker entered the bathroom and found the Arabs chain on the floor. He got excited and said, "I'm going to quit now. I'm rich!"

Julio told Cisco what he heard and called for a meeting with the rest of the gang.

COLOMBIA

Jose Luis was with his wife and Mono, enjoying the day on their five-million-dollar yacht and relaxing on the waters off the Caribbean sea. They were eating fresh seafood that their chef cooked for them. His wife Margarita raised a cup of wine. "Cheers to life and the joys it brings."

Jose Luis raised his glass. "I could cheer to that. I have a surprise for you."

"Really, you know I hate surprises."

"Well, you should get used to it by now because I love looking at the expression on your beautiful face when I shower you with diamonds, houses, cars, and anything your heart desires." As their boat named *Dreams Come True* docked in the port of Barranquilla in Colombia, their hometown, Jose Luis grabbed his wife's hand and helped her off the yacht. They headed toward a commercial vessel just a few feet from where his yacht was docked at. There were workers starting to unload different sizes of crates from the vessel onto a truck. Jose Luis walked over to the truck with his wife. They climbed aboard and Jose Luis grabbed a tire iron. He popped the top from one of the crates then put his hand inside and took out a gold rooster.

Margarita said, "Oh, how beautiful."

"Yes indeed, and very pricey twenty-four-carat gold," said her husband. They got off the truck and walked over to their Rolls Royce where the driver opened the back door for them to get in.

Margarita asked him, "What clsc is in those crates?"

He smiled, winking his eye, "Everything to make a gold house."

ECUADOR

As Jose Luis and his wife were getting driven home, he called his associates from Ecuador. George Guerra was one of his partners whom Jose Luis trusted. George was in charge of running the cartel's activities, mainly shipping tons of cocaine to other nearby Latin American countries, which were then bound for European countries. "Guerra, como estas?"

George Guerra was in his pool talking to Jose Luis, "Hey, Jose, I'm good. How is the wife?"

"She is here with me. We just got off the boat. We were out sailing for the day. Now we're heading home. Listen, George, I found out a way you could send me money undetected. You're going to love it when you receive a package from me then you're going to know what I'm talking about, okay. When you come, I tell you more about it. See you in a few days."

"Very well, until then, amigo." A few of George's men gathered around his pool. George's head of security Alex told two of the men to get undressed and jump in the pool. The two men did what they were told and entered the pool. They swam to the middle of the pool where George was. The only thing sticking out the water were their heads. George told them, "Now that I know nobody here is being recorded, we are free to talk. How many tons of cocaine can you handle in a month?"

PANAMA

Ricardo Lopez was another one of Jose Luis's international partners. He was responsible for the cartel's money laundering and distribution across the Panama Canal. He was on a yacht with his family and friends off the coast of Panama, enjoying the fireworks and celebrating a public holiday in acknowledgment of their country securing independence from neighboring Colombia. He was familiar with the ins and outs of the Panama Canal, which stretched 48 miles and connected to the Atlantic Ocean. Panama City was the forty-sixth most dangerous cities in the world. The capital city saw 543 murders in just under a year, which the Bandidos Cartel were accountable for more than half those murders due to the execution of rival drug gangs who were trying to tax the usage of remote drug routes in jungle-controlled territories. Panama City was a well-structured city in most aspects, resembling major cities across the world, but outside of the city mirrored much of Central America that parts the coastal line were remote with rough access to the city.

Drugs originated from countries like Colombia and Venezuela lie directly to the south. Panama and Colombia shared a jungle- entrenched border, which did not have a major road connecting the countries. That's how Jose Luis drug cartel, the Bandidos, moved tons of drugs freely through the thick jungles and then by sea where larger loads could be moved quicker. Ricardo commanded a military-run training camp with young local rebels who murdered other narco groups trying to rob the cartels for drug shipment boosting up the murder rate in that country.

Jose Luis was on the phone with his trusted commander and partner. "I'm hearing a lot of bodies are popping up. That's bad for business. The government there is going to be a problem for us if we continue to be careless."

"That's why I build a cement pool."

"For what?"

"When we meet, I will explain. Send the G-5 for me."

Jose Luis was getting out of his Rolls Royce. "Okay, start packing."

MEXICO CITY

Fernando Garcia was a Mexican drug lord that had a bounty on his head for five million dollars. The Mexican and US government were aware of his ties with the Bandidos organization. He was responsible for overseeing the main hub of distribution for Jose Luis's cartel. He played a key role in the cartel's global trafficking which required strategically penetrating customs' borders undetected. For the last three years, the primary method of transporting their cocaine was through large submarines that were capable of carrying one hundred tons at a time with a street value of over four hundred million dollars. To avoid capture, he won't sleep in the same house twice. And all his hideouts were equipped with underground tunnels that connected to other neighboring homes. He was even known to disguise himself as a priest living in a church at times. Fernando traveled with a small heavily armed army, ready for any confrontation from local cartels or military government's police who were looking either to capture or kill him on sight.

When he was not in Mexico, he was in Guatemala, receiving large shipments and coordinating various methods of transportation back to Mexico and onto US soil. Usually Fernando be on a fishing boat fishing and sailing along the coast of Guatemala, looking out for customs' boats and spy planes to inform an incoming sub. Where a few hundred miles toward Colombia, there be submarines hovering along the ocean floor underwater for weeks with a crew of four, usually a captain, an engineer, a seaman who helped steer and unload the cocaine, and another personnel who was there to make sure the cargo wasn't diverted or didn't disappear. The particular self-propelled submersible vessel came with a hefty price of one million dollars. It was equipped with water-cooled mufflers to reduce heat signal. It was not fully submerged, but it skimmed the sea's surface, moving quickly at night then drifted like sleeping whales during the day under the cover of darkness. They slither out of Colombia's shallow rivers, and ten days later rendezvous off shore along the Central American coast, usually near Guatemala where the cocaine was unloaded onto recreational or fishing boats then the subs were sunk.

COLOMBIA

Jose Luis purchased four G5s so his close associates and partners could travel the world in style, comfort, and undetected from customs. The G5 landed on a private strip and stopped alongside Jose Luis's identical G5. George Guerra flew in from Honduras. He was handling business there, paying off high-ranking military personnel who were on the cartel's payroll. When he landed in Colombia, he got on a Wrangler Jeep and was followed by two more Jeeps with armed men escorting him to a safe house off the mountains of Colombia.

Another G5 landed on the same private strip next to the other G5s. Ricardo Lopez traveled from Panama to see his boss. A short time later, Fernando's plane came in from Mexico and landed next to the other G5s. As he approached Jose Luis's estate, armed guards let them pass. He exited a black Suburban dressed as a priest with a few armed men. Around the perimeter of the house were more armed men patrolling with assault rifles. Inside were the leaders of the cartel, George, Ricardo, Antonio, and Fernando. They all stood up and greeted their boss as he made his way down from the top of the stairs with his monkey.

"Gentlemen," he said in Spanish, "I'm happy you all made it safely." He told everybody to sit down. As a maid was pouring him a drink of Cognac, he lit up a cigar. He waited till the maid left and continued to say, "The reason I called this meeting is because you could only say but so much on a phone.

"You're right about that," said George.

"How are things in Ecuador, George?"

"Well, I did what you told me to do. I spent two million building clinics, schools, and soccer fields for the locals kids since the government in those remote areas don't give a shit. So we have the support of the

---

92

villagers there. We have at least twenty labs up and running in and around the villages."

"And you think twenty labs are enough for a global demand of 500 to 800 tons annually?" Jose Luis asked.

Antonio added, "We do have another fifteen labs in Colombia."

Jose Luis asked, "Did you order more diesel engines?"

Ricardo answered, "Yes, I have." Ricardo oversaw the manufacturing of their fleet of narc-submarines. The logistical capacity required in order to have a skilled engineering team to take massive materials into the heart of a vast jungle, including heavy equipment such as prolusion gear and generators were not easy tasks. Sometimes they were put together in pieces and then reassembled in other locations under the jungle trees and in camps outfitted with sleeping quarters for workers. Some subs cost as much as two million each and took a year to build. The design and manufacturing techniques employed in their construction had improved over time. They were faster and more seaworthy. An 18-meter-long narco sub could reach speeds of 18 km/h and carry up to ten tons, typically made out of fiberglass powered by a 225–260 diesel engine and manned by a crew of four, carrying large fuel tanks which gave them long range of 3700 kilometers and were equipped with satellite navigation systems. The vessels were nearly impossible to detect via sonar for radar and were camouflaged with blue paint. Ricardo answered his boss, "We have ten diesel engines in stock."

"Order another ten." Jose Luis turns his attention to Fernando. "Fernando, how are things? Are you limiting the horrific violence that is terrorizing that country?"

"No, the problem is getting worse. There is a bloodbath going on with the other cartels."

Jose Luis got up, "More bodies, more problems, this is just no good for business."

Ricardo told his boss, "Build cement pools."

"Cement pools. What the hell you mean, Ricardo?"

"I build a cement pool and fill it up with acid. Then I throw all the dead bodies in the pool. Everything dissolves. No face, no case."

Jose Luis clapped and told everybody, "Okay, you see there's a solution for every problem. Let's start building acid pools. Fernando, start selling to all the cartels in Mexico so they could eat too. And those who don't pay, don't kill them. Throw their family in the pool. That way, they know we mean business.

"Antonio, what is happening down over in Puerto Rico? Do you know Puerto Rico has a 3.6-billion tourism industry annually? We are raking in over five million dollars a year, legit money."

"That's why we invested five hundred million in commercial properties. We have two of the best hotels in the island."

"Yea, but I can't have a war between local drug gangs raging nearby. Call a meeting. Tell them we want to pay protection then when you have them all in one place, kill them all and throw them in the A- pool."

Fernando got up. "Boss, we are losing one out of every five cargos. We have to give the Guatemala/Mexican routes a break."

Jose Luis took a pull from his cigar. "Antonio has new routes off the Caribbean Coast."

Antonio explained, "We are going to start sending submersibles from the Caribbean Islands reaching Puerto Rico. There's 311 miles of coast line we could penetrate without detection. We purchased five new fishing vessels to assist in unloading the subs off the Caribbean shores. We just got to watch out for the CBD."

Jose Luis asked, "Who?"

"The Custom and Border Protection. Them pigs got that Dash-8 aircraft hovering at night, flying 3500 feet above our Caribbean prime smuggling routes, the Mono Passage. Their radar system is sensitive enough to detect patches of sea grass floating on the ocean surface and an infrared camera powerful enough to zoom on a vessel seven miles away. They know we have eyes watching them fly off the runway in Aguadella, Puerto Rico so they fly off at different times. We alternate routes by island hopping through St. Martin up through the Virgin Islands. It costs a little more, but the loads get in without getting intercepted. As far as the weapons are concerned, we still use sea but also freight, private couriers, and US Mail. Basically, whatever it takes. We have a strong presence down there. We equipped our guys with AK-47s and AR-15s with extended magazines, scopes, lasers, and armor-penetrating *cop killers*."

Jose Luis said, "That's good to know for them other traffickers trying to take over territories. Just don't forget to build a pool up in the mountains."

On a another note everybody take a look around you. Have you not notice the twenty-four carrot gold tables. The chairs you are sitting on are twenty-four carrots. Everybody was impressed. Jose Luis said, "I'm building a gold Rolls Royce too. Fuck these banks holding my money."

MANHATTAN, NEW YORK

Ken is driving around looking for Cisco. He drove to all the places he hung out but had no luck finding him. He called him but his phone was off. Ken headed over to Lynda's house. When he got there, he sat on her couch and watched as she came out in a sexy red lingerie.

"Do you like?"

Ken got up and walked toward her. He lifted her up. "Do I like. You know how to make a man go crazy." He carried her into the bedroom and lay her gently on the bed. She started to take his shirt off and kissed him passionately on his lips. Then she unstrapped his belt and wrapped it around his neck, pulling him closer to her as she started to pull his pants down.

He got in bed with her and started to roll around the bed, holding her tight. They kissed and made love. In the morning, Ken woke up and saw that Lynda was not lying next to him. He screamed, "Babe!"

"I'm in the kitchen cooking breakfast. Hope you like pancakes and bacon?"

"Hell yea!" He started to think about his sister lying in the hospital and his friend Muller, who died, and when he went to the funeral.

Brooklyn, New York

Abdul's cousin Mohammad told him that their good friend Wisam was found dead in the bathroom of the club. Somebody robbed him for his chain. "It must have been drug addicts," Abdul said. "Can't wait to kill them all."

Abdul's cousin asked him, "Can you trust those drug dealers you getting ready to do business with?"

"Relax, my brother, we will be ready for them." They passed by the Barclay Center and entered the mosque where they prayed. An hour later, they came out with a couple of men.

Julio's wife Sheila and Cisco's wife Tamika were in a restaurant waiting for their husbands to come so they could have dinner. They were getting a drink by the bar. Sheila told Tamika, "This fool thinks I'm stupid. He comes in whenever he wants to. Then he want to pipe me raw. Shit, I don't know where he been. One day, he came drunk. I pulled his pants down, and, girl, let me tell you, it smelled like a fish market."

"Wow, I would've chopped it off. I don't play that shit."

"Trust me, I thought about it."

Julio and Cisco arrived at the restaurant. They parked across the street in an indoor parking lot then crossed the street and went inside to eat. Undercover agents were half a block away, keeping surveillance. After they ate and kissed their wives good-bye, Julio told Cisco, "Come on, let's go. The boss is waiting for us."

Instead of going out the front, they left out the back and hailed a cab. When they got to Juan Carlos's house, the first thing Juan Carlos asked was if they were sure they weren't followed. Julio said, "No, we used the eat-and-leave-out-the-back move."

They started to drink and play pool. There were women running around in bikinis, flirting with the men. Julio told his boss about Abdul's crazy plan to buy three hundred keys and wanting to spike the drugs.

Juan Carlos scratches his head. "I don't get it?"

Julio went on to say, "He wants to poison the cocaine to kill people."

Cisco said, "Who cares what he going to do with the shit as long as we get ours. Money is money."

Carlos replied, "That bastard is crazy. You know the type of heat that will bring to the organization.

Julio agreed, "Yea, you talking DEA and even Home Land Security, and what about the drug addicts? If you kill them, then who the hell is going to keep buying our shit."

Cisco said, "Well, if we don't sell it to them, they just going to go somewhere else."

Juan Carlos replied, "That's why you going have to kill that piece of shit when the deal goes down. And after you kill him, all of yous can split the money."

Julio said while smiling, "Now that sound like a nice plan. Ain't that right, bro?"

Cisco yelled, "Hell, yea!" They all grabbed their drinks and made a toast.

"To free money," Julio said. He grabbed a female and carried her into a room and closed the door. He left his phone on the table that was vibrating. It was his wife Sheila.

The next day, Abdul was in his house on his knees praying. His wife Hindah made him some lunch, and after prayer, he told her, "Today another phase of the plan is about to unfold."

She looked at him with a worried face. "Abdul, please be careful."

He hugged her and kissed her on her forehead. "I will." He then went over to the pile of money on the floor and started to put it in a duffel bag. He made a call to his cousins who were at another location, arming themselves. They were loading up their weapons, looking at the news. The newscaster was commenting on Syria and the ongoing crises.

Rahan said, "Don't worry. I'll be there soon to help." The cousins grabbed their weapons and put them in laundry bags and headed out the door. They picked up three close friends and arrived at Abdul's house. He came out with a large duffel bag full of money. His kids ran out the house behind him. His eldest son Wali asked if he could go. And Abdul told him his time had not come yet to serve. But when his time came, he would be ready to fight against the Western crusaders. He kissed his sons and got in the van. They drove by the Barclay Center and got on the highway to go meet with Julio.

In the van, Abdul put on a bulletproof vest. Two of Abdul's cousins Rahan and Mohammed plus three of their friends from the mosque, Zakar, Nameer, and Ismail were in the van armed with AK-47s. Abdul drilled the men and told them, "We must be ready for these immorals. If things go wrong, shoot till you have no more bullets. Kill till there are no more bodies standing."

Juan Carlos texted Victor to go to the storage and bring three hundred dollars for the light bill, a code message which meant three hundred keys. A short time later, he arrives with the merchandise in a van. Julio came out of a house with Cisco and told Victor, "Come on, I might need you too to hold us down."

Victor told him, "For what? I don't get paid for holding people down."

"Well today, you are going to get paid. How about a little ten racks for one hour's work?"

"What you waiting for, let's go. My son could use some of that for his college books and part of his tuition." Victor called his son Jayden. He was at home in front of his computer, doing research for a project. Jayden was an eighteen-year-old college freshman. He was a clean kid who stood away from drugs and gangs. He wanted to become an engineer. His mother was separated from his father because she found out Victor was cheating on her.

Julio called his eighteen-year-old cousin Hector who was coming out of school and walking his girlfriend home. He picked up his cell phone. "Hey, Who, talk to me, baby."

Julio asked him if he wanted to make some quick cash. Hec said, "That's what I've been waiting for, man." Julio gave him an address and told him to meet him there right away. "Say no more, on my way." Hec kissed his girl and told her he had to go to do something. "When I come back, I'm going to get you some new boots, okay? Because them shits you got on are leaning, can't have you walking like that with me, baby."

Abdul got to the location where the deal was supposed to go down. It was a five-story building that was used to park cars. The van he was in made its way up to the fifth floor. He told everybody to get in position. All the men got out of the van.

Hec paid the cab and got off in front of a building that was an indoor parking lot. Victor pulled up to the building and let Hec in the van. He told Julio, "What going on, fam?"

"Everything good, sonny. You ready to get this money?"

"Hell yea, born ready, baby."

"Just do as I tell you. We be out of here in less than ten minutes. We going to rob this dude for some bread." He handed Hec a gun.

"That's what I'm talking about. You going to see, my nigga, I'm gangster."

Victor drove into the parking lot building up to the fifth floor. Julio and his men exited the van.

Abdul came out from behind a car with one of his cousins. He saw Julio, Hec, Cisco, and Victor. "Julio, I see you have brought people I don't know or ever seen before."

"Relax, you know Cisco, and this is my little cousin Hec and Victor. I trust these people with my life."

"Trust, it's hard to find nowadays."

"Yea, I know. Well, I trust you brought the money?"

"What, you think I came to play games?" He motioned to his cousin Rahan and told him in Arabic, "Get the money." Rahan went behind a car and pulled out a duffel bag. He brought it in front of Abdul and opened it.

Hec saw the money and walked over to it.

Cisco asked Abdul, "Is it all there?"

"Of course, it's all there. Now where's my shit?"

Julio screamed, "It's in the van. You want to check it out?"

Abdul told his cousin in Arabic, "Go see." Cisco opened the door from the van. When Rahan went to look inside the van, he saw the bricks and opened one. He tasted it and waved at Abdul. Then Cisco came from behind and put a gun to the back of his head.

Cisco told him, "Stay cool, don't say a word, or I'm going to blow your fucking head off."

He disarmed Rahan. Abdul screamed to his cousin to bring the drugs.

Julio said, "There's been a change of plans. We confiscating this money. Seems like you're crazy ass want to cause havoc and chaos to our billion-dollar business. I fucking chop your little ass to pieces before you carry that dumb plan out."

Cisco came out with Rahan, holding a gun to the back of his head. Hec pulled out his gun. "Game over, clown. Run that bag!"

Abdul screamed, "You really want to play games, ass hole!"

Victor saw from the corner of his eyes toward the right side a trunk of a parked car slowly opening up. He screamed, "It's an ambush!" He fired off one round from his weapon, striking Abdul in the chest. Abdul's friend Ismail came from around a parked car that was by Abdul and started shooting toward Victor who ducked under a truck. Hec froze. The trunk of a Chevy car opened up and Abdul's cousin Mohammed started shooting rounds from his AK-47 at Hec. And on the opposite side of the Chevy across from where Mohammed was shooting, Abdul's friend Nameer opened the trunk of a Buick car and started letting off rounds from his AK-47. The crisscross barrage of bullets caught Hec, hitting him on his right and left side. The only thing that was keeping Hec up were the bullets that were penetrating his body from both sides. Abdul, who was shot in the chest, was dragged behind a car by Ismail as he was shooting at Julio. Victor emerged from under a truck and shot Nameer in the torso, killing him instantly. Rahan tried to run away from Cisco. Cisco shot him in his ass and hid behind a car as Abdul's friend Zakar was shooting in Cisco's direction. Then Julio let off a barrage of bullets toward Rahan, killing him as he fell out of the fifth-floor window, landing on a busy sidewalk.

Julio screamed over to Cisco to go and get the money. But Zakar was shooting at Cisco.

Cisco told Julio, "I can't. These mother fuckers are all over!"

Mohammed jumped in the van where the drugs were and sped off, hitting Victor who went up in the air. Mohammed stop the van. Zakar was shooting at Julio while Abdul threw the duffel bag in the van and jumped in. Zakar tried to get in the van, but Julio shot him in the back, killing him as the van sped off down toward the ground floor. Abdul got away with the drugs and the money. He plucked out a bullet from his bulletproof vest and kissed it. Cisco stopped a car that was coming down from the sixth floor. It was a lady with her kids in the back. He forced her to get out and drove the car in reverse with her kids in the back until he got to where Julio and Victor was. They got in the back with the two kids as Abdul's friend Ismail was shooting out the back windows. Cisco backed up the car, hitting Ismail dragging him backwards and crashing the car into a wall, smashing out a fifth floor window where Ismail flew out of. He was still letting off his weapon in the air as he fell, landing on a hot dog truck below and died. Cisco put the car on drive and headed down to the next level where the mother of the kids was standing in his way. He stopped the car in front of her. The little boys were crying in the back of the car. The frantic mother was standing in the middle of the fourth floor, screaming, "Please just let my kids go, or you going have to run me over!"

Cisco asked Julio, "What I do?"

Julio smacked Cisco in the back of the head. "Man, give that woman her kids." Julio opened the back door to the car and told the kids to get out and go calm their mother down.

Cisco drove up to Mark's driveway who was a childhood friend of Julio. Mark heard a car horn and came out the house. He went over to the car and asked Julio, "What the hell's going on, man? You sounded crazy on the phone. You know I'm on parole, man. Don't do this to me, bro."

"Shut the fuck up and help me get this nigga in the house." Mark looked around and helped Cisco get Victor out the stolen vehicle. Julio told Cisco to get rid of the car.

Inside, Mark asked, "What happened to him?"

Julio told him, "He got hit by a car. Listen, we just got robbed. I ain't had nowhere to go."

"What do you mean you just got robbed!" Mark came back from the kitchen with a pair of scissors to cut Victor's pants.

"That shit got crazy. They got us, man." Mark tried to raise Victors leg to see if it was broken.

Victor screamed, "It hurts."

Mark cleaned up the scrape marks. He asked Julio, "What you got robbed for?"

"Wait until this nigga finds out," Julio says, shaking his head.

Mark gives Victor a bottle of Hennessy. He looked at Julio and asked him, "Wait, to who, find out what?"

Julio peeked out the window. He told Mark, "The boss, man, they just got us for three hundred keys."

Mark's face went pale. "What, yo, man, get the fuck out my house, man!"

Julio screamed back, "Oh, it's like that now, cocksucker. When your wife was playing you and was here fucking that nigga, who the fuck you call to help you when her side squeeze pounded you out that night. You forgot when you came home and busted him digging your wife's back out on your own bed, and then he threw your coward ass out! Who was the one that came and put two bullets in his head and one in that nasty whore then drove to the bridge and threw both of them off it while you stood in the car crying like a little bitch. Now go roll me a joint you coward."

Juan Carlos was in the bathroom, soaking in a Jacuzzi and watching football on a TV screen. He was smoking a cigar while a young blonde woman was pouring him a glass of champagne. His cell phone rang. The blonde female handed him the phone. "Julio, where the fuck you been. I've been calling everybody. Nobody pick up and where the fuck is Victor?"

"Victor is with me. Listen, boss, we got robbed for the shipment."

Juan Carlos jumped up and spilled the drink on the blonde. "I don't want to hear that! You better go out there and find my shit you dumb bastard!" Juan Carlos slammed the phone down. He shook his head. "These motherfuckers can't do shit right."

Victor asked, "Well, what he said?"

Julio turned on the TV and went through the channels and stopped when he saw news on the shootout he was just involved in. "What you think he said. He mad as hell. Look at this shit" as he pointed at the TV. There was a news truck on the scene. The TV was showing two dead men on the sidewalk who had fallen out from a five-story building with one of them landing on a hotdog truck.

Mark said, "Unbelievable."

Victor was moving his leg. His knee was swollen from when the car hit him. He was starting to feel tipsy after taking of few sips from the bottle of Hennessy Mark gave him to alleviate the pain. Victor said, "I don't know how we got out of there alive."

Julio shook his head. "Maybe it wasn't our time to go."

Cisco was under a bridge, burning the stolen car they highjacked. He had to make sure he destroyed it. He couldn't afford for police to link him and his crew to that gun battle that left a gruesome crime scene with a half dozen bodies lying around. He called his wife Tamika to come pick him up. When she arrived, she also brought along federal agents who were staking her house out in hopes Cisco would show up. They followed her right to Cisco.

Tamika told Cisco she was worried about him. "I got a bad feeling something is going to happen to you."

Cisco kissed her, "Relax, baby, we got enough money to move and start a new life. Just give me till the end of the week, baby."

She whispered in his ear, "Just keep in mind streets have an expiration date."

Tamika dropped off Cisco back at Mark's house.

Federal agents called in and told their commander, "Sir, we followed the target's wife, and she led us right to him."

Franconia said, "Keep him under tight surveillance and don't let him get away this time, you morons."

Avenda was home in her room packing a small traveling bag. She called the number Yousef gave her. The Syrian man on the other line told Avenda to meet him at the bus terminal in downtown Manhattan on 47th street at 4:30p.m. She told him her friend was going with her.

"The more the merrier." He said.

She went over to her mother's room and saw that she was sound asleep. She left her a letter, stating that she was leaving for Syria to join her fellow brothers and sisters. "Do not worry, Mother, for I shall be in the care of God. I will call you as soon as I settle in. I love you." She signed, "Your daughter, Avenda." She placed the letter on her mother's dresser and left the apartment.

On the bus, she called her friend Asma and told her to hurry up. She was going to be there in ten minutes.

"Okay, okay, I meet you downstairs." Asma's mother Fariah was finishing washing clothes in the basement laundry room of her building. She called her daughter to come and help her fold the clothes. Asma was grabbing clothes from her dresser and stuffing it in a small luggage. She looked at her parents' picture that was on top of her dresser and put it in her bag. She wondered if she was doing the right thing in accompanying her best friend to Syria. Since school was over, she thought of just going for the summer. Her mother was calling her on the phone, and on the other line, Avenda was also trying to reach her.

Asma's father Farhan told his wife Fariah, I'm going to start bringing up these clothes that are already folded and stay upstairs to make us lunch." Fariah told her husband to tell Asma to come down. He headed for the elevator and when it arrived, he got on. Asma left her house and was waiting for the elevator upstairs. Avenda was calling her on the phone. So she decided to take the stairs to make time. Her father got off the elevator as Asma opened the door to the staircase and walked down the stairs. Farhan opened the door to his apartment and yelled for his daughter, but there was no answer. "Where did she go?" he wondered.

Downstairs, Asma met Avenda. She told her, "I don't know if I really want to go."

"Please, we talked about it already. We're going to watch each other's backs. I can't thank you enough for coming with me."

"Like I told you, Avenda, if it don't feel safe, I'm coming right back."

Avenda grabbed her hand, "Don't worry. We're going to be all right." They headed toward the subway station.

UPSTATE, NEW YORK

Abdul and his cousins Mohammed, Nazar, and Zyan were pulling up to a house in a wooded area in up State New York. He specifically rented the house because it was in a secluded area away from neighbors. They entered the house carrying bags, boxes, along with three metal containers that Nazar used a hand trunk to roll in the house. Inside, Abdul told Zyan to place the bags and boxes on top of a long table. Abdul started taking out the contents of what were in the bags and boxes. There were glassware, test tubes, plastic funnels, storage bottles, burner stands, laboratory utensils, a chemical test kit, aprons, gloves, and a few gas masks.

"Here put these on," Abdul told his cousins, pointing to the aprons and gloves. He told them, "Hey, be careful with those steel drums," which contained salicylic acid, hydrogen peroxide with fluoride acid. He instructed Zyan to grab the box which contained aluminum hydroxide powder and put it on the table.

His cousin asked him, "All this stuff looks dangerous. What is in this bag?"

Abdul explained, "That is batrachotoxin. It is a poison made from frog excretions. The frogs themselves don't produce the toxin directly but through digestion of melyrid beetles the frogs eat. Pass me that dioxin."

Zyan passed his cousin the bag. "What does this do?"

"That causes skin lesions, but I don't know if I'm going to use it yet. The defecation of internal organs and bleeding till the body is dried out is more than enough internal destruction for any human body to endure. Yea, by the time I finish mixing these chemical agents together, I'm going to feel real sorry for the people who sniff or inject this cyanide. You know what I don't see here, go back to the van and get the antifreeze and bleach and the press machine, Mohammed."

Nazar was looking at Abdul's notes. "What is cytotoxicity?"

Abdul explained, "That is the degree to which a chemical agent or toxic material possesses a specific destructive action on certain cells." Abdul put on an apron, gloves, and gas mask. He turned on the table burners and started mixing the chemical agents together and slowly started processing the toxic liquid fluids into a dry powdery substance. Nazar then transferred it to large plastic containers using funnels. Abdul asked Mohammed to bring him a brick of cocaine. Abdul weighed one thousand grams of the deadly substance and started to mix it with the drugs, making it into two bricks. Abdul said, "It is now time to test this and see if I did everything right." Abdul sent Nazar and Zyan to go and get him a victim.

Manhattan,
New York City

Avenda and Asma arrived at the 42nd Street bus terminal. She called the Syrian man and asked him, "Where is Yousef?"

"I'm his uncle. I'm running a bit late. I be there shortly."

Avenda told Asma, "We have to wait. Let's get something to eat." They sit at a coffee shop and buy two bagels with two cups of chocolate. After they ate, Asma's cell phone rings. "Okay, I meet you by the bathroom," she said. "Come on, Asma, he is waiting for us." Asma's phone rang. It was her brother Iman.

"Where are you? Mom and Dad are worried about you. Why you don't answer their calls?"

"I'm going on a trip."

"A trip, what you talking about?"

"I'm leaving with Avenda to Syria. Tell them I'll be all right, okay. I will call home when I arrive."

Iman screamed, "Are you out of your mind!" She hung up on her brother.

"Come on, Asma, you're walking too slow. He is calling." Finally, they met the Syrian man.

He said, "How you doing. Are you Avenda?"

"Yes, and this is Asma the one I told you about."

"Okay, come on. The bus is about to leave."

"Is Yousef going to meet us?"

"Yes, when we arrive." Asma's phone started to ring. She saw it was her brother, but she didn't answer. They were on a line, getting ready to get on the bus. The Syrian man got on the bus along with Avenda and Asma.

Iman texted Asma and said that their mother passed out when he told her that she was going to Syria. "She had a heart attack. Please come home. Don't do this to Mom." The door of the bus closed. Asma told Avenda she couldn't go because her mother fell ill. Asma told the bus driver to let her off the bus. She hugged Avenda and told her good luck. Avenda told her, "You have to grow up one day." The Syrian smuggler tried to grab Asma's hand as she was getting off the bus. She kicked him in the groin and got off the bus.

Asma headed home.

Upstate, New York

Nazar and Zyan drove into town and saw a young female walking her poodle. Zyan drove up to the woman, and Nazar jumped out with his gun out. He ordered the female to get in the van. She quickly picked up her dog and ran. Nazar chased her into someone's backyard. She was yelling, "Help me. Help me!"

She tried to climb a 5-foot fence, but Nazar grabbed her leg and dragged her down. She kept screaming for help. Zyan hit her over the head with his gun, and she lost consciousness then Nazar threw her over his shoulder. The poodle bit Nazar in the leg. He kicked it to the other side of the yard. The owner of the house, an old man came out with a shotgun. He told Nazar, "Hold it right there. Drop the gun and put her down."

Nazar dropped his gun and put the girl down. The old man said, "You know you're on private property, boy. That means I got the right to shoot and kill you."

Zyan sneaked up behind the old man and shot him in the back of the head and said, "So do I." As they were driving back to the house, the woman woke up.

She started to cry, "Please don't hurt me. I'm pregnant!" Zyan told her to shut up. When they reached the house, Abdul was waiting eagerly with the garage door open. Zyan pulled in and Abdul closed it. They took the screaming woman out and dragged her into the house. Abdul took a small portion of the venomous drug and poured it in a needle. The abducted girl was crying as Nazar was holding her. Zyan whispered to Abdul, "She said she is pregnant."

"Really, how convenient. We're getting two for one."

As Abdul approached her, she started to scream, "What do you want? Call my husband. He'll give you anything you want."

Abdul told her, "All I want is your honest opinion." He then stabbed her in the arm with the needle. Abdul was watching her with anticipation as he injected the poisonous drugs into her veins. Zyan let her go, and she fell to the floor. Then her eyes started to roll back. As she gagged, foam started coming out of her mouth. Abdul's cousins were shaking their heads, smiling. The female was on the floor gasping for air. As she lay there, she started to bleed out of her eyes, nose, mouth, and ears. Then she started to defecate her arteries and intestine. As she gave her last breath and died, she had an abortion. After that, her liver and heart were all pushed out her rectum. Abdul's cousins started to throw up. Abdul screamed, "Yea, it works. It works. I'm a fucking genius!" He told Zyan, "Clean this mess up and put what's left of her in one of them drums that still has acid in it."

Zyan looked in disgust. "You're serious? It stinks."

Abdul told Mohammad to get the press machine ready. Abdul had a custom press with a logo that read Cyanide and had a design of a scorpion with two tails on it. He wanted it stamped on every brick to make it look like it originally came from the cartel he robbed the shipment from.

Manhattan, New York City

Ken was turning into Tenth Avenue, the block where the DEA building was located. It started to rain. He turned his wipers on. He heard a woman across the street, screaming because a man snatched her purse. As the purse snatcher ran toward Ken, he opened his car door, causing the thief to hit his door and fall to the ground. Ken immediately sprang into action, got out his car, and grabbed the thief, preventing him from leaving the scene. He had to wrestle with the lowlife as another cop came and handcuffed the criminal. Ken took out his badge, making it visible so the cop could see he was also an officer of the law. The lady whose purse was snatched came over to Ken and thanked him for not letting the purse snatcher get away. A police car came and took away the man who was in handcuffs. Tamika, Cisco's wife was driving by and saw Ken. She couldn't believe her eyes. She tried calling Cisco, but the battery from her phone died. Ken got back into his car and proceeded to head into the DEA building. Agent Romo was doing a brief hearing on the drug cartel. There was a roomful of old and new narcotic agents. Ken sat down and listened in as Romo was pointing at a screen on the wall where there was a pyramid set up with all the ring leaders of the cartels whom the DEA was diligently going after. On the top of the list was four top lieutenants of the Bandidos Colombian Cartel. "George Guerra, who controls distribution in Ecuador, our resources claim he heads a narco army that protect their labs and drug routes from other neighboring countries. Ricardo Lopez, stationed in Panama, he navigates tons of drugs out the Panamanian Canal. Pedro Feliciano, a mexican drug lord who directs and controls everything that moves from Guatemala to Mexico City and over our borders. Then we have Antony Quiñones, very low key individual from Colombia. He heads a team of engineers that have technical capabilities and intelligence to build submersible vessels. We are in the next generation of smuggling conveyance. Narco mariners are evading prosecution with submersibles that are equipped with technologies that make them difficult to intercept. Even though our US forces use state-of-the-art submarine warfare strategies against them. Most are slipping through our net. These men are spread out from Colombia, Panama to Ecuador and Mexico. The ring leader is rumored to be Jose Luis Rios, The ruthless drug lord along with his top commanders run there operation like an army. Out of Colombia, they are processing approximately thirty thousand kilograms of raw cocaine base into cocaine powder, resulting in four hundred tons every six months and reaping tens of billions of dollars. We are in close communication with our international partners who are close to bringing the gang to justice. They are the big fishes who distribute via land, air, and sea. The organization also employs hit men who allegedly carry out hundreds of acts of violence including murders, kidnappings, tortures, and violent collections of drug debts at the orders of their leader Jose Luis Rios. All were indicted by a federal grand jury with the help of a confidential informant who helped Agent Hernandez, who at that time was posing as a dock inspector. There were multiple secret indictments issued out, but no one has been brought to justice yet. Unfortunately, the CI and Agent Hernandez were assassinated."

Ken's phone rang. He jumped out his seat when he heard it was Cisco on the other line.

"Hey, Johnny, it's me, Cis." Cisco was at the carwash, looking for a specific car scent as he was waiting for his car to be washed.

Ken walked out the room. "Where the hell you been? I thought something happen to you!"

"I lost my phone. This is my new number, bro. Yo, a lot of shit's been happening."

"What you talking about?"

Cisco continued, "Look, man, I know this shit might sound crazy. This dude tried to buy three hundred keys from us and wanted to poison the drugs to kill as many addicts as possible."

Ken interrupted Cisco, "Who the fuck would want to do that? He trying to fuck the game up?"

"Yea, that's what the fuck my boss said. Anyway, we wanted to rob him for the buy money and kill his monkey ass, but he wound up having the upper hand. Instead, that bastard ended up robbing us for the coc, man."

"No, you joking."

"Do it sound like I'm fucking joking, man! We looking for this motherfucker now."

"What's the guy's name. Maybe I know him."

"I'm going to send you a picture."

Ken asked Cisco, "Where you at, so I could help you find him?"

"I'm moving around. I'm going to text you an address to meet up later, okay?"

"Yea, do that." Cisco hung up. Ken went back into the room and interrupted Agent Romo. He told everyone, "We got more problems. There's another player we need to focus on." Ken received a text message form Cisco that read, "Yo Johnny this is the dude. His name is Abdul Malik." His face was also attached to the text. As Ken was speaking, he plugged his iPhone to the screen monitor, and Abdul's face popped up. Ken went on to say, "Apparently, this looks like a homegrown cell who is plotting to unleash a chemical attack by way of poisoning a quarter ton of cocaine in an attempt to wipe out the entire addicted population."

The commander said, "Not a bad idea."

Agent Romo laughed out loud. "Then we be all out of work."

Franconia replied, "I don't give a rat's ass. I'm retiring next year."

Agent Carter asked Ken, "How reliable is this information, Ken?"

Ken pointed to Cisco's face, "Reliable enough to start issuing search warrants for the Hermones Drug Gang."

Agent Romo ran Abdul's name through their criminal database. He looked in astonishment "What do we have here." They got a manhunt out for him already. "You heard about it, that terrorist group that robbed the Delaware Bank just last week. They were responsible for killing eight Delaware police with a dozen hostages."

Agent Ramsey said, "Wow, they almost wiped the whole police force out. How did they do that?"

Commander Franconia replied, "They were using drones with machine guns mounted on them."

Agent Romo said, "This is getting very interesting." Ken placed Abdul's picture along with his accomplices next to the drug cartels. The commander told Ken, "It's time to bring in Cisco and see if we could flip him. We certainly have enough on him to put him away for life. Hey, Romo, get on the phone with Home Land. Let them know what's going on with Abdul Malik. They need to be looking for his ass too."

"Yes, sir, right away." Ken left the room and headed out to bring Cisco in.

Julio, Victor, and Mark were at a pool hall. A waitress named Jena, who Julio used to bang, brought him a drink and asked him, "What's the matter, boo? You look stressed out."

Julio took the drink. "I got ninety-nine problems but a bitch ain't one."

"So if females ain't your problem, then why don't you come pick me up after work. Whatever it is, I'm sure I could get your mind off it." She grabbed his crotch.

"That sounds good as long as I'm still alive."

Four men dressed in black hoodies, black jeans, and all wearing black Timberland boots approached Julio. "Got here as fast as we could, my man, you ready?" one of the men named Rock asked.

Julio got up and gave him a hug. "Thanks for coming, Rock. Come on, we got some hunting to do." He kissed Jena on the lips, "I call you, mamita." All seven men left the pool hall and got into a black van with tinted windows.

BROOKLYN, NEW YORK

They drove pass the Barkley Center then kept going down to where a mosque was and waited across the street to see if they see Abdul. Then after waiting around for over an hour, they decided to ride around.

Julio told Rock, "Stop the van! That kid over there in that funny orange sweat suit, he looks like one of those punks that was with Ab in the club. Let's get that little cockroach!"

Rock and his goons approached Abdul's cousin Nazar. They snatched him and put him in the van.

He screamed, "What the fuck you want with me, man!"

Julio put a gun to his mouth, "Where you about to go is to hell, and you're going to burn there till you tell me what I want to know." They drove to Mark's house, and the men dragged Nazar into the house's basement.

He told the men, "I don't know nothing, man. And if I knew, I wouldn't tell you shit!" Rock chained him to a water pipe on the ceiling. Nazar was hanging from the pipe with just his underwear on. Rock started to beat Nazar with an electric wire.

Julio asked him, "You still don't know where Ab is?"

Nazar spits in his face. "Go suck a pigs dick."

Julio took a cooking pan that was on the table and hit him over the head with it. Julio asked Mark, "Go get me an iron." Julio told Nazar, "Listen, I don't know who you are. I don't care who you are. But if you don't start talking, I'm going to use your face as an ironing board."

Mark plugged the iron to an extension cord and plugged it to the wall. He handed the hot iron to Julio. Nazar looked at the iron. "What are you going to do with that? You crazy. My cousin going to kill you all. We deep, man."

Julio screamed, "Deep!" He pressed the hot iron to the side of Nazar's face and yelled, "Deep! I'm going to keep going deeper if you don't tell me where the fuck that clown is!"

Nazar was screaming from the pain. Julio took the iron off his face. "Where is he?"

Nazar said, crying, "If I tell you, he is going to kill me."

Cisco screamed, "And what the fuck you think we going to do to you!" He starts to place the iron to Nazar's ear, pressing hard and burning off his ear which got stuck to the iron.

Nazar screamed, "He is in a house in Upstate New York, 2260 Greenland Road!"

Julio told Rock, "Drop him and put him in the truck."

Mark, googled the address. "That's about an hour away."

Cisco went to the bathroom to take a crap. Julio called his boss and told him, "Finally, that little monkey cracked."

Juan Carlos was getting a massage by a young girl while another one was slowly stripping her clothes off, dancing erotically in front of him. "That's good. Now maybe I could get my shit back."

"Yea, I had to sizzle his ear off. I hit you when I get there."

"Text me the address. I meet you there. I want to make sure he don't get away this time."

"Okay, boss."

Cisco called his wife Tamika. She answered, "Hellow."

"Hey, baby, I'm going to be home a little late. I got to handle some business." As he was getting up to wipe his ass, he saw there was no toilet paper, so he grabbed the display towel hanging on the wall.

"Devon, where the hell have you been? I've been trying to call you. You got to get home now. I have to tell you something real important. You're not with Johnny, right?"

"Relax, what you talking about?"

"Johnny's a cop. I saw him earlier." Cisco locked the door to the bathroom. "Tamika, are you crazy?"

"No, I'm not. Just get home so I could explain it to you that motherfucker is a cop."

Julio knocked on the bathroom door. "Yo, bro, what you doing, taking a shit. Hurry up. We leaving."

"Be right out." He told Tamika, "I be right home."

When Cisco got upstairs, Julio saw him sweating. "What's wrong with you? It looks like you seen a ghost or something."

"No, it's just hot in here."

Nazar was in the corner with his hands tied behind his back. Cisco went over to Nazar and kicked him in the face. "You little bastard, you try to kill me."

Julio told Cisco, "Relax, we still need him around just in case he's lying about that address." Cisco spits on Naza. Julio told everybody, "Come on, let's get out of here."

As they left the house and were getting in the truck, the feds were taking pictures, reporting in to central command. "Sir, we have a visual on everybody. Do we take them down now?"

The Commander asked, "Is Juan Carlos with them?"

"That's a negative."

"Just keep surveillance on them to see if they lead us to Juan Carlos."

"Roger that, sir."

Cisco stood outside the truck and told Julio, "Yo, bro, I'm going to get some more firepower at the house. And bring some bulletproof vests. Shit look like another gunfight. I don't want none of us to get hurt, okay."

Julio stared. "Hurry up then. I meet you up there. I want to make sure he don't get away."

"For sure, man." He asked Mark to lend him his car.

Mark threw him the keys. "Take it easy with her. I just got her."

Julio laughed. "You know what they say when you lend your car out. It's like lending your girl. They going to fuck her hard."

Cisco smiled and told Mark, "Don't worry. I'll treat her like she was mine."

Julio laughed harder. "You see what I told you."

Cisco got in Mark's Mustang Cobra convertible and drove off with the feds following him in an unmarked car. Julio got on the highway with the rest of the gang as the feds were following them in a dark blue minivan with black tints. All Cisco could think of was how Johnny could be a cop. He thought about the day Johnny sold him a brick of coke and how he sold him ten bricks another time. "It can't be. It can't be," he told himself.

As Cisco is driving up to his driveway, his wife Tamika and his daughter Natalie came running out.

Tamika told him hysterically, "Please tell me you never did nothing with Johnny?"

Cisco picked up his daughter, Natalie, "What are you talking about?"

"Johnny, I saw him downtown with a badge hanging on his neck."

Cisco put down his daughter. "What the fuck you talking about?"

They went in the house. Tamika told Natalie to go play in her room. Then she asked Cisco, "What's up with your phone? I've been calling you, and at first, it was ringing then it went out of service."

"I lost it. Tamika, where you said you saw Johnny?"

"I was downtown coming from a conference meeting that my job wanted me to attend. Then as I was about to get on the highway, he was in the middle of the street, arresting someone."

"Are you serious?"

"Devon, why would I lie about that."

He started to think about the key of coke Johnny sold him. "It can't be. He sold me a key. Then I sold him ten keys. Oh, my god, are you sure it was him? You probably confusing him with somebody else."

She disagreed, "No, I'm positive. I put my life on it, baby. If you did do business with him, you're in deep trouble."

Cisco starts to shake his head. "No shit, we got to get out here before he come looking for me."

"He already has."

"Yea, when?"

"Yesterday and he was anxious."

Cisco ran to his bedroom. He went into his closet and took out a gun and three Nike shoe boxes that were full of one hundred dollar bills stacked to the top. Tamika came in the room. He told her to get her jewelry and get Natalie ready.

She asked, "Where are we going to go?"

Cisco started to put the money in a knapsack. "I don't know. We figure it out. Let's just get out of here." Cisco's phone rang, but he didn't pick it up. He told his wife, "It's him. Get Natalie and let's get out of here." Cisco grabbed the gun, the money bag, and his wife's jewelry box.

When he opened the front door of his house, he saw two undercover cops approching the front steps who told him, "Devon we need to talk to you." The officers tried to rush into the house but had to duck for cover when Cisco let off two rounds from his 9 millimeter pistol. Cisco slammed the door of his house and ran toward the back of the house. He opened a back door, leading to the backyard and ran out.

Ken was waiting for him with his gun out, yelling, "Stop, Cisco, it's over!"

Cisco turned around with a gun in his hand and took a shot at Ken. Ken returned fire, hitting Cisco. "You motherfucker," Cisco said before he fell into the pool. Hundred dollar bills started to float in the pool.

Tamika ran outside and jumped in the pool to help Cisco. She was screaming, "You fucking pig, why you had to shoot him?" The pool was turning red from Cisco's blood. Natalie came out crying, "Daddy, Daddy!" The undercover agents grabbed the little girl. Ken went to the edge of the pool and helped Tamika pull out Cisco who was bleeding from a gunshot wound to the shoulder, he was going in and out of consciousness. All Cisco kept telling his wife was that he was sorry.

Upstate, New York

Abdul and his cousins loaded the venomous narcotics onto a van. He doubled his quantity to more than half a ton of the deadly drug. The plan was to move the drugs closer to the city to distribute them quickly and swiftly before the panic broke out. Abdul opened the garage door, letting Zyan out. Mohammad stood behind with Abdul to help clean up. A short time later, Rock's van drove up close to the house where the terrorists were. Moments later, Juan Carlos arrived. Julio told him he was waiting for Cisco that was bringing more firepower.

Juan Carlos told him, "How many men you need to take out this little monkey. I got four men. You got six men."

Victor was in the back of the truck with a swollen leg. "I can't do shit, man. My leg is fucked up. It's too swollen to put weight on it."

Juan Carlos stuck his head in the truck. "Do what you do best, drive. Just watch this little rat. If he try to escape, shoot him," Juan Carlos passed him a gun.

Ken was watching the drug gang through a pair of binoculars as agents were positioning around the perimeter of Abdul's house. Aside from the DEA, agents from Home Land Security were there to assist in capturing Abdul and his accomplices. In addition, Captain Trevor was also there with his department and a SWAT team. Ken said, "I got a visual on Juan Carlos."

Agent Romo came over. "The choppers are almost here."

As Juan Carlos's men were approaching the house, a raccoon was sniffing around the garbage cans, making noise. Abdul was inside with a gas mask on, disposing the rest of the dangerous chemicals. Mohammed heard a noise. He grabbed his AK-47 and peeped out the window. He saw a few men approaching the porch of the house. He led off a round from his weapon, shattering the window and killing one of Juan Carlos's men. The others ducked behind a few garbage cans, positioning themselves while firing back into the house. As one of the men was reloading his machine gun, he looked down and saw he was kneeling on a dead raccoon who was caught in the gunfire. Victor ducked down in his seat when he saw cops creeping by the van he was in. He told Nazar, "Don't make no noise. If I hear a fart, I'm going to shoot you in the back of your head."

When Abdul heard the gunshots, he grabbed his weapon. Mohammed ran past him saying in Arabic, "They're all over. Let's get out of here."

Both men ran towards the back of the house with their gas mask still on. Julio ran in the house, shooting at Abdul who ran out the house and jumped in the pool to duck for cover. Mohammed ran in the back of a Jacuzzi as Juan Carlos came around the house shooting at him. Bullets hit the Jacuzzi, causing it to leak water out. One of Rock's men ran toward the pool but Abdul jumped out of the water and let off multiple rounds, killing the man instantly. Four Agents snuck up on the back of Juan Carlos's men and started shooting at them. The hit men hid behind the pool bar. Beer and liquor bottles were bursting in the air from bullets that were coming out of Ken's machine gun. He screamed, "This is the DEA, put down your weapons. We have the place surrounded!"

Mohammed let off a few rounds toward Juan and Julio, enabling Abdul to get out off the pool and run towards his cousin. Then they ran into the woods. Captain Trevor and his agents were shooting toward Julio's men, killing one of them whose weapon jammed. Julio and Juan Carlos ran after Abdul and Mohammed who were running down a steep hill. Mohammed fell and rolled down the hill. He was shooting up at Julio and Carlos. Captain Trevor radioed to Ken and Romo that four of the suspects ran into the woods.

Ken radioed back, "We're onto them!"

Julio's men were shooting at Homeland Security, Swat and local police killing a half dozen law enforcement. The captain was shot in the arm. He shot back and another one of Julio's men went down. A member of the SWAT team stormed the house. Shooting in the dark, he shot a propane canister and the house blew up.

The blast injured and killed a half of dozen officers, along with Jaun Carlos men. Rock ran into the pool on fire. Victor attempted to flee when he heard all the gunfire. But when he was trying to get to the front seat, Nasar tried to grab his gun. Both men were wrestling for the weapon when it went off, killing Nazar. When Victor got to the front of the van, there was no key. He yelled, "Shit! Shit!" He looked out the window at another truck that was there and crawled toward it. He saw the keys in the ignition. He got in and sped off. Abdul and Mohammed ran into a dirt field where there were people racing their Off-Road UTV four-wheeler cars. Two kids who were racing down a hill in their four wheelers had stopped to use the bathroom. Abdul and Mohammed leaped out the bushes and jumped on one of the four-wheelers and sped off.

Juan Carlos and Julio came down from the hill, shooting at Abdul who was shooting back as they drove off, blending with a group of riders, and disappearing into the wooded dirt trails. The chopper had trouble seeing them because it was a wooded area. When the owner of the other four-wheeler came out the bathroom, he ran back in when he saw Ken and Romo running and shooting toward his four-wheeler car, which Juan Carlos and Julio stole. As they sped off in the direction of the terrorist, Juan Carlos was shooting his machine gun at the agents.

Ken saw a UTV heading his way. He waved at him, ordering him to stop. He told him he needed his UTV.

The man said, "Are you crazy?" But when he saw Ken's badge, he got off.

The agents rode off into the dirt trails, chasing the suspects. Mohammed was driving the UTV through mud up and down the dark dirt trails. Abdul was shooting back at Julio while Juan Carlos was shooting back at them. Then Ken joined in on the shootout. Julio was ducking his head as bullets were zooming by him. As the terrorist were riding in the woods, Abdul pointed to a woman riding a Jet Ski/ATV on the lake that stretched alongside the dirt trail. Mohammed then rode over a hump, and the UTV went up in the air as Abdul was shooting at Juan Carlos and Julio. The UTV landed into the lake in front of the woman who was heading toward them. Abdul let off a round out of his machine gun and killed her. Juan Carlos and Julio stopped at the end of the dirt trail, shooting at the lake as Mohammad yanked the dead woman off the Jet Ski/ATV into the water. Both men got on the watercraft. As thy sped away, Abdul was on the back, shooting at the drug dealers. When Ken and Romo got to the end of the dirt trail, another shootout erupted. While Juan Carlos was shooting at the Agents, Julio ran out of bullets then jumped in the lake and started to swim underwater, trying to get away. Juan Carlos was behind the four-wheeler, still shooting at Ken who returned fire, killing the leader of the drug gang. Ken radioed to the chopper to track the criminals from the air. They radioed back, saying they had an acrial view on the suspects. The terrorist were coming to the end of the lake and flipped a button on the Jet Ski and the wheels popped out, converting it back to an ATV as they drove it onto the wooded land, disappearing again from the chopper's view.

Victor was inside a gas station, paying for gas. He walked over to the truck and started pumping gas. `Abdul and Mohammed crossed a road and incidentally headed toward the same gas station Victor was at. They crept up behind him and put the machine gun to his head.

Abdul said, "You look familiar."

"So do you. Oh yea, you that crazy Arab who robbed us for them keys."

Mohammed said, "And you that dumb fool who tried to rob us for the buy money."

Abdul asked, "You finished pumping gas? Now get in the truck." As they drove off, Abdul told Victor, "I have a once-in-a-lifetime proposition for you. You could retire from this. You want to hear it?"

"Do I have a choice?"

Manhattan, New York City

Ken rushed over to the hospital. When he got to his sister's room, his parents were around Jessica, crying. Ken's mother told him that a blood artery ruptured in her brain, and she went into cardiac arrest, losing oxygen from her brain, and now she is living thru a respirator.

Ken screamed, "No!"

His father grabbed Ken who started to cry on his shoulder. "Why, Dad, why did she have to get worse?"

His dad was patting him in the back, "I don't know, son, I just don't know."

His mother was asking, "God, why did you take her from us. She was my little angel." Then she passed out. The next day, Ken was at his parents' house. Jasmine was cooking in the kitchen. Ken asked her, "Hey, Jaz, where's my Dad?"

"Hi, Ken, I think he is in the backyard."

Ken went out to the yard and saw his father siting on a chair. "Dad, you know why I'm here."

His dad turned around. "Yes, I know, but your mother doesn't want to do it. She doesn't understand."

Ken put his hand on his father's shoulders. "If we wait for her, Jessica would never be buried and rest in peace."

"I'll talk to her."

Jasmine came out. "Dinner is ready. Ken, you're staying, right?"

"Of course, how can I miss them juicy meat balls."

The day of Jessica's burial, a lot of her colleagues from the department came to the funeral. There was a gun salute with the American flag lying on top of her coffin with a beautiful bouquet of red and white roses. Her family was around the coffin in tears as Father O'Neal said a prayer on behalf of Jessica. Ken's mother was holding on to Ken's arm, wiping the tears from her face. When the funeral was over, Captain Trevor came over to her and gave the family a hug.

The next day, Ken was at the prison where Cisco was being detained. Cisco was in the hospital ward, recuperating from a gunshot wound to his shoulder. The guard brought him out and handcuffed him to a chair. A short time later, Ken entered the room. Cisco told him, "Well, well, well, you're the last person I would expect to see. You have some nerve coming here."

"You should be eager to see me. I'm probably the only one in this world that can help you. The type of time your facing is not looking too good for you. You know how the game works. The more you tell the less you get."

"My father always told me snitching is for cowards."

"What are you, twenty-five? You probably get out in twenty years with good behavior. That would put you at forty-five. And your little girl will be what, twenty-eight? Is that what you want?"

Cisco looked up at Ken. "There's nothing you could do for me."

Ken leaned forward. "Not if you tell me where Julio Mendez is. You see all these charges you're facing, I could talk to the prosecutor to reduce a substantial amount of time. Who knows, maybe you'd be out when you're around thirty-five. I know you heard about your boss Juan Carlos Santos. He is dead. The last one standing is Julio. Once he is in, he can never get you because we're going to make sure he never comes out. So you're starting to see how all this could work in your favor. Just cooperate and I will promise that you will see your daughter's teenage years."

Cisco thought about the time Julio told him never to flip on him at the jewelry store when he brought him that Rolex. Cisco looked up at Ken. "Is that going to be in ink?" Ken pulled out a paper and slid it over to Cisco with a pen. Cisco started to think of his daughter Natalie and his wife Tamika. He then asked Ken, Can his lawyer look over it?"

"Sure, in the meantime, tell me where can I find Julio?"

Cisco told Ken the places Julio could be. "One more thing, Cisco, did Julio ever mention to you about shooting those cops and the K-9 in that January raid?"

Cisco answered. "He used to brag about it all the time."

Ken got on his motorcycle and left to look for Julio. He had three places to check where Cisco told him he might be able to find him. After checking a few places and no signs of Julio, Ken checked his list and headed over to the last address Cisco gave him. When Ken arrived, he saw it was a pool hall. He entered and went over to the bar and ordered a beer. There were a few people playing pool. When the bartender brought him a beer, Ken asked him where he could find Jena.

"May I know who is asking?" Ken pulled out his badge. The bartender asked, "Is she in trouble?"

"No, but you are if you don't tell me where she is."

"She's off today."

"Where does she live?"

"I don't' know. You could ask the manager. His office is in the back."

"Thank you." Ken went to the back and knocked on the manager's door.

The manager said, "Come in."

Ken entered the office with his badge visibly hanging from his neck. The manager was a gay man in his early thirties with long black hair. He asked, "How can I help you?"

"I need to find Jena. I understand she is not here today."

"No, she's not. It's her day off."

"Can I get the address to where she lives?"

"Oh, I'm afraid I can't do that. It's confidential. If you want, you could leave me your card, and when I see her I let her know you were looking for her."

Ken went around the manager's desk and grabbed him by his hair. "We could do this two ways, either you tell me where she lives or I beat the shit out of you."

The manager yelled, "Okay, you don't have to be so rough!" He rummaged through a drawer at the bottom of his desk and pulled out Jena's information.

Ken snatched the paper from the managers hands. "See that wasn't so hard, right?" Ken left the pool hall and headed toward Jena's house.

Julio's clothes were spread out in Jena's house, leading into her bedroom where she was having sex with him. Her cell phone was on the living room table, ringing. It was on vibrate, and the call is coming from her job at the pool hall. The manager was trying to call her to give her heads-up that a cop was asking questions about where she lived. After they made love, Julio got in the shower, and Jena went to the living room to get a cigarette from her purse. She saw it was a missed call from her job. She wondered if they were trying to reach her to come in on her day off, so she decided not to call back. Her phone rang again, and she still didn't answer it. Then she received a text from her job, saying that a police officer was looking for her. She called her job and the manager told her a cop was asking where she lived and from the look of it, he was heading over there mad.

Jena told the manager, "Shit, I wonder what they want with me. I paid that ticket for drinking in public last month."

The manager said, "Girl, that don't look like it was for a ticket. It looked more serious than that."

"Okay, thanks for the heads up. I'll see you tomorrow."

Ken was almost at the address that he read on Jena's job application. Julio came out of the bathroom in a towel. He asked Jena, "What's wrong with you?"

She lit up a cigarette. "I don't know. Some cop was looking for me at the pool hall."

"What, did they give the cops your address?"

"Yea, supposedly, they are on their way."

Julio panicked. "Oh shit, I got to get the fuck out of here." He quickly put his clothes on and ran out the door.

Jena screamed, "Don't forget to close the door behind you, you crazy bastard!"

Ken was turning into the block where Jena lived. Julio was already on his bike, starting it up. He rode off with Ken in pursuit. Julio saw through his side mirror that somebody was behind him. He started to go faster on his motorcycle. He raced down the street, and when he saw cars in front of him that had stop to wait for the light to change, he jumped on the sidewalk. There were two cops standing on the corner who saw him speeding toward them with horrified pedestrians running for cover.

Ken also hopped on the sidewalk. The patrol cops standing in the corner saw Julio approach them. He popped a wheelie, and the officers got out of his way. Ken had to suddenly swerve to the right to avoid hitting a little girl who came running out of a store. As he approached the two cops on the corner, one of them hit him with their nightstick on his helmet.

Julio jumped on another sidewalk and went inside a park where there were little kids playing. Parents were scrambling to grab their kids so they wouldn't get run over by the reckless motorist. Ken followed Julio into the park. A patrol car was cruising down a three-lane street on the other side of the park when Julio rode out the park and onto the street.

The cop who was driving said, "What the hell. This guy's high."

Julio rode right by him then did a wheelie and sped off. The officer put on his siren and started to chase Julio. Then Ken sped by the cop.

The cop said, "No respect."

Julio rode onto a one-way street. Cars were blowing their horns as Julio was speeding toward them. Ken was right behind him. The officers had to give up the chase because oncoming cars were blocking them from entering the one-way street.

Julio raced down the street. People were looking in disbelief as he sped by them at dangerously high speeds. Then he rode down into a railroad yard, trying to get away from Ken. A train was coming, and Julio was riding alongside it with Ken behind him. There was a wall up a head, and Julio was trying to beat the train to cross over and avoid hitting the wall. With nowhere else to go, it was a do-or-die situation. Ken started to go faster to also beat the train so he wouldn't crash into the wall and safely cross over. If he didn't make it, Julio was going to get away. The train was nearing the crossing where there was a brick wall on its right side, the wall Julio wasn't trying to hit as he and Ken got closer. Finally, as the wall was nearing and both bikes were doing over 150 miles an hour, Julio and Ken managed to narrowly pass the speeding train by inches crossing the tracks and avoiding crashing into the wall. A bum was pushing a cart full of junk out of the train yard and as he emerged from the end of the abandon building, Julio crashed into the bum's cart. Julio went up in the air and landed on a garbage can that was lit on fire to keep other bums warm. Julio was on fire rolling on the ground. Ken got of his bike and ran toward Julio as he grabbed a blanket from a bum. He then started to hit Julio with the blanket. Ken put out the fire and took off Julio's helmet.

Julio's face was burned on one side. He told Ken, "I knew you was a pig from day one."

"You should have gone with your guts, and that's exactly where I'm going to shoot you. This is for my sister Jessica, Muller, and her partner Sammy you lowlife filth." Ken shot Julio five times in the stomach. Julio spat blood out his mouth and died.

Abdul and Mohammad drove up to Zyan's building in the Lower East Side. They parked and went upstairs with Victor. Zyan was watching TV when his cousins arrived. Zyan asked, "What's he doing here?"

"Relax, Victor is going to help us distribute the drugs. I mean really spread it out from state to state all the way down the East Coast. In return, I will spare his life, and he also gets to keep the proceeds from the sales."

"He can't beat that offer."

"Yea, he would have been a fool not to take it."

Mohammad laughed and said, "Yea, a dead fool." Abdul was looking at the news. The news commentator was elaborating on a recent shootout. "State and federal officers were involved in a shootout with a drug gang and a terrorist group who were being investigated. Police stormed a house in the Upstate area, the suspects were using the location as a lab to mix destructive chemicals and launch a chemical attack. We have dead officers and suspects on the scene who have been killed in the raid. We are following this story as it unfolds to keep you updated." Zyan turns off the T V. Victor got a call from his girlfriend Teresa. She told him her friend Tamika called her, telling her that her friend, Lynda's boyfriend Johnny, was working with the feds. "He was the one that brought everybody down. Victor, be careful."

"Good, looking for that info." He hung up his cell phone and told Abdul, "There is a federal agent by the name of Johnny who is coming after all of us."

"Really, does she know where to find this Johnny to kill him?"

Victor got back on the phone and called his girl, "Hey, babe, you wouldn't happen to know where that cop's girlfriend lives?"

"No, but I know where she works. Do you want the address?"

"Yea, text it to me." Victor told Abdul, "We're going to have to go where she works."

"Come on, let's go."

Brooklyn, New York City

They headed over to the salon. When they got there, Lynda was already closing the store with another employee. They watched as she got in her car and followed her to her house. Lynda drove a short distance and pulled into her driveway. She entered her house and went in the bathroom to turn on the shower. She undressed and was in her panties, combing her hair in front of a mirror and putting it in a ponytail. She then took off her panties and got in the shower. Victor and Abdul along with his two cousins were in front of Lynda's house. Victor picked the lock, and they all entered her home. Abdul went to the front of the bathroom door. He heard the water running and the voice of a singing woman. He motioned to the others, pointing at the bathroom door. Mohammed opened the door and saw Lynda through the plastic shower curtains. He pulled the curtains, and when Lynda saw him, she started to scream. Mohammed grabbed her and put his hand on her mouth, preventing her from screaming. He took her out the bathroom and threw her on the bed. She grabbed a towel on top of the bed to cover herself. "What do you want? I have money in my purse if that's what you want. Just don't hurt me."

Abdul pointed a gun at her. "I'm not here for money. Just do what I ask and you won't get hurt, is that understood?"

"What do you want?"

Victor threw her the house phone. "Call your boyfriend Johnny boy and tell him to hurry up and come because you fell coming out the shower, and your ankle is swollen. And if you dare to say anything different that will alarm him, then we're all going to rape you before shooting you. Do you understand?"

She shook her head yes and started to cry. She dialed Ken's number.

Ken was at a bar, having a drink thinking about his sister and pumping those five bullets into Julio. His cell phone rang and he saw it was Lynda.

He picked it up. "Hey what's up, babe." With Abdul pointing a gun to her head and Victor licking his lips, she went on to tell Ken," Hi, honey, you not going to believe this, but silly me, I slipped coming out the shower, and I twisted my ankle. It's real swollen. Can you please stop by and bring me some ice pads?"

"Wow, you okay?"

"It just hurts so much. Could you please come?"

Ken told her to stay off her ankle that he'd be right there.

Abdul took the phone from her. "You did good. Now we wait."

"What you want with him? You're not going to hurt him, right?"

"No, I just want him to check something out for me."

Victor asked her, "Is there anything to munch on? I'm starving." He went to the kitchen, opened the refrigerator, and took out a piece of cake.

Ken was driving his motorcycle up the driveway. Zyan saw him through the window. He told Abdul, "Show time." Abdul told Lynda to stay lying on the bed and call Johnny into the room when he comes in the house.

Ken saw the lights from the house on. He rang the doorbell twice. He then opened the door that was unlocked. He went inside and yelled, "Lynda, where you at? I brought you the ice pad, and I got you a bottle of wine, babe!"

"I'm in the bedroom."

When Ken entered the room, he asked, "Why're you in here with the lights off?" Mohammed turned on the lights, and Ken saw Abdul on the bed with a gun to Lynda's head.

She told Ken, "Sorry, they forced me to call you or else they were going to kill me."

"Did they hurt you?" Victor came from behind and unarmed Ken. Abdul told his cousin to tie him up.

Ken said, "Abdul Malik." Then he turned and looked behind him. "Victor Alvarez?" Then he saw Abdul's cousins. "And Usman Mohammed with his brother Zynan Alijaber."

Abdul told Ken, "I see you know everybody here, which leads me to believe you know too much."

Victor said, "Yea, and that's scary."

Ken looked at Abdul. "Let her go. She has nothing to do with this."

"I'm afraid that's not possible." Abdul shot her in the forehead.

Ken screamed, "No, you crazy motherfucker. I'm going to fucking kill you!"

Abdul laughed. "Not if I kill you first."

Abdul looked around. He went into Lynda's closet and took out an ironing board. He then yanked a telephone cord from the wall and puts the ironing board behind Ken's back as he was wrapping the cord around Ken, tying him to the ironing board. Then Abdul went over to the kitchen and pulled out two clear half-inch wide rubber twenty inch hoses from the refrigerator that were connected to the water fountain on the door. He then started to look in her kitchen drawers for duct tape which he found and went back into the bedroom. Abdul told his cousins, "All right, grab this pig and bring him here to me." Abdul was standing at the corner of the room by a radiator steam pipe that ran from the floor to the ceiling.

Ken was asking, "What the fuck you doing?"

Abdul said, "You'll see." They lined him up upside-down and tied him to the iron steam pole. Then Abdul duct-taped Ken's mouth and stuck the two clear rubber hoses into his nostrils so he had no choice but to breath out of them. Next, Abdul taped the hoses to Ken's nose, securing it tightly and making sure they won't come out of his nostrils. At the other end of the twenty-inch rubber hoses, Abdul taped a plastic cup with a whole in the middle. As he looked up, he saw a wall speaker. He climbed on top of a dresser and duct-taped the cup to the top of the speaker. He told the guys, "Now here comes the fun part." He took out a plastic bag that was full of the poisonous drugs he contaminated from his pocket and poured it into the cup with the hole in the middle.

Victor said, "Wow, you are a crazy motherfucker."

Abdul told everybody, "Come on, let's get out of here. We got work to do."

They left Ken tied to an ironing board upside-down with his mouth duct-taped and two skinny rubber hoses taped to the inside of his nostrils, so he had no choice but to breathe through the tubes. The tubes were duct-taped along the wall up to a cup with a whole in the middle and full of Abdul's venomous drugs. As Ken breathed in through the tubes, the powdery substance started to trickle down, getting closer to his nostrils. Ken looked up to where the plastic cup was and told himself, "What have I got myself into?"

A short time later, he started to think how it all started, his sister lying in a coma then burying her. How he asked his childhood friend Peter to let him use his store as a front and how he met Lynda, and because of him, she was dead.

Victor was in a van with Abdul and his cousins. They were waiting for one of Julio's customers who controlled the Brooklyn area. Victor tells

Abdul, "Whoever thought my boss and my whole crew would be dead, and now I'm teaming up with your crazy ass."

"Let me correct you. You're teaming up with your new boss. Don't get it confused you work for me now." Travis came up to the van.

Victor told him, "Get in."

Travis got in and said, "Yo, Vic, what up, sup with everybody? Nobody picking up their phones." He looked at Abdul and his cousins. "And who the fuck are them?"

"Don't worry about them, they my peoples."

"Yo, man, sup with Julio. I got his paper."

"Julio is on vacation."

"I'm fucking dry. What's going on? I got this dude that want two, another nigga that want four. They blowing my phone up."

"I got you, my man, there's fifty keys there. Everything is back to normal, just flood the streets."

"Oh word, that's what's up. Yo, Vic, I got three hundred thousand there that belong to Julio. You want to give it to him?"

"Yea, he asked for that."

Travis got out of the car. "It's in my trunk. Come get it." Victor got out the van and went to the back to give Travis the contaminated drugs then went with Travis to get the money. Then Victor got in the van and drove a few miles to another location. He stopped in front of a carwash and waited for Butler, another one of Julio's dealers. He opened the door from his van and pulled out a duffel bag full of keys and handed it to Butler. Meanwhile, Travis was in his stash house selling four keys to a Jersey customer who got on the George Washington Bridge heading for New Jersey.

Peter went over to a bar where he and Ken went often to play pool. He asked the bartender if she had seen Ken. "He was here earlier but left in a hurry. I think he went to his girlfriend's house, something about she fell and hurt herself."

"Really." He tried calling him to see if he wanted to come back to the bar to keep him company but got no answer.

Ken heard his phone ringing that fell on the floor, but he couldn't get to it because he was tied up. Ken could see the spiked drugs dripping down the rubber hoses, getting closer and closer to his nostrils as he inhales through his nose.

Peter was at the bar sipping on an apple martini and texting Ken. He wrote, "Kenny you getting your pee pee wet. I know you in Lynda's house. Damn, I got kicked out of my own house. Nyla is too jealous. She argues about everything. Anyway, when you read this, hit me back. I'm at the bar." After drinking a couple of drinks, Peter left the bar and drove off. He passed by Lynda's house and saw Ken's bike parked outside. He tried calling him again, but he didn't pick up. Peter told himself, "They probably sleeping. Let me go to a hotel."

Ken was sweating profusely. The white killer powder was inches away from his nostrils. He started to think how they were going to find him tied up, upside-down and dead. And when the autopsy returned, it was going to read, "Died of a drug overdose." He started to laugh. "At least, the department was going to tell my parents I died trying to save the world, putting my life on the line, and trying to prevent a bio-chemical catastrophe, only to be captured by the enemy and forced to inhale this crap. Wow, it makes for a good movie. Only no one saves the super hero. What a fucked-up ending." Tear drops fell on Ken's cell phone.

Peter was driving away when he saw two teenage thugs sitting on Ken's bike thru the rearview mirror, taking pictures. He backed up and got out of his car and told the teenagers to get off the bike.

One of them said, "Relax we was just taking pictures" then they walked away. Peter wondered why Ken would leave his bike out like that. He looked up at the sky, and it looked like it was about to rain. He decided to go and knock on the door to wake up Ken and tell him to put his bike away. Peter rang the doorbell, and Ken heard the bell. The powder was a half-inch away from his nostrils. He had been holding his breath for the last two minutes. Peter kept ringing the doorbell. He turned the knob to the front door and opened it. He walked in and yelled, "Hey, Ken, it's Peter! Lynda!"

Ken heard Peter but could not yell back because his mouth was taped up. Finally, Peter saw the light from the bedroom. He walked into the bedroom and saw Lynda on the bed. As he walked over to her, he saw she had a gunshot wound on her forehead. He said, "Lynda, holy shit." Ken heard his friend Peter and started to shake the ironing board to get his attention. Peter heard a noise coming from the corner of the room. He walked over, pulled the curtains, and saw Ken who was practically blue. Peter said, "What the fuck" and yanked the tape off of Ken's mouth. He screamed, "Is that a bomb!"

Ken mumbled, "Get that shit out my nose."

"Who did this? Are you all right?"

"Yea, I'm all right, just get me down and untie me."

Peter helped Ken down. "What happened to Lynda?"

After Peter brought Ken down and untied him, Ken hugged Peter. "Thanks for stopping by." He went over to Lynda and knelt by her bed and started to cry. He told Peter, "They killed her for no reason, and it's all my fault."

Manhattan, New York City

Ken was at the DEA office along with agents from the DHS and NBIC. Vivian Thomson, who was head of the National Biosurveillance Integration Center, led a team of experts whose mission was to enhance the capability of the federal government to rapidly identify, characterize, localize, and track a biological event of National concern. Also to integrate and analyze data relating to human health, animal, plant, food, water and environmental domains. The team was called in to assess the internal damage and magnitude of the situation. The three different federal departments, all were watching the news coverage of what appeared to be a biochemical invasion on US soil. They stood stunned, observing countless addicts suffering the consequences upon consuming the contaminated drugs. Many of the drug addicts were showing up dead, lying on sidewalks, restaurants, subways, buses, and cars. All of the local hospitals were flooded with dead people who died from blood leaking out of their noses, mouths, ears, and eyes prior to their death. Vivian, along with her staff, was shocked and in disbelief as they were witnessing a biological attack unfold on the citizens of New York. A news cameraman was filming in the streets of Manhattan when a distraught elderly man who just finished shooting up a bag of Abdul's poison came running out of his house toward the cameraman screaming for help. He was bleeding heavily from his eyes and nostrils and screaming he couldn't see. Then the old man's pupils popped out as more blood gushed out his eye sockets. The cameraman ran the other way. The driver of a garbage truck opened a bag of cocaine that was labeled Poison and sniffed it through his nostrils. A short time later, the garbage truck crashed into a house because the driver was leaking blood out of his pupils.

The helper who was behind the truck came around asking the driver, "What the hell is wrong with you, are you drunk?"

"Help me!" the driver cried.

His helper looked shocked at what he saw. "Oh, my god, what happened to your eyes? They're bleeding, and they look like they're going to pop out of your head!"

The driver yelled back, "I don't know, man, that shit I sniffed is fucking me up!"

"What shit?" The driver started to roll violently on the ground as blood started to leak out of his nose. He got up and charged toward his co-worker, yelling for help. The helper started to run away from the truck driver, screaming, "Stay the fuck away from me you zombie!"

Three armed robbers entered a grocery store and robbed the owner at gunpoint. When the bandits exited the store, a fourth accomplice was waiting in a getaway car outside. The owner of the store grabbed his shotgun and ran out the store, shooting and killing one of the robbers as he was trying to get in the car, which sped away, leaving the dead bandit on the street. Police officers who just so happened to be patrolling the area witnessed the robbers fleeing the scene. They started to chase the suspects, but the cop who was driving the patrol car started to bleed out his nose and eyes. His partner looked at him and screamed, "Oh, my god, what the hell is happening to you?"

"I don't know. I can't see." Then his partner lost control of the car and jumped on a crowded sidewalk. People who were walking on the sidewalk started to run and get out of the way. Some of the pedestrians got ran over. Then the car crashed into a pump and came to a halt.

The head of HLS, NIBC, and the Anti Terrorism Department (ATD) were in different vehicles, looking for the terrorist group. They had a folder with the terrorist faces attached to a profile sheet. One agent said, "This guy Abdul was on our terrorist network watch list but dropped off the radar. He has been linked to different radical groups and Yemen jihadi extremist afflicts. In the last five years, he has traveled to France, Lebanon, Afghanistan, and Yemen."

Another agent in the car said, "And now he is here causing havoc." As they looked out the window, stuck in traffic, a man on a bike crashed into their truck. He was bleeding out from his mouth, nose, and eyes. He was knocking on the window, smearing blood on the windshield, and begging for help while holding one of his eyeballs in his hand.

New Jersey, Newark Airport

A private plane was at the airport lifting off. The pilot of the G5 started to bleed from his eyes. Him and the stewards were previously getting high. He made a sudden U-turn, and the workers at the airport tower saw the plane flying in their direction. The stewards ran out the cockpit, screaming that her eyes were burning. Blood was gushing out her eyes. Passengers were freaking out and a panic broke out. The captain's eyes started to bleed, and he started to yell, "I can't see!" His eyes popped out of his head and got stuck to the front windshield of the plane. The jet crashed into the control tower, exploding and killing everybody aboard the plane and in the control tower.

Over at the Raway Maximum Correctional, Prison Corrections Officer Greg Brady was starting his shift. As inmates were serving food the officer started to sneeze out blood from his nose onto one of the inmates plate of food. The inmate got up from his table, saying, "What's up, man, that's some real nasty shit!"

Then Officer Brady kept sneezing repeatedly in the direction of the inmate, splashing blood all over his face. Officer Brady started to scream, "God, my nose, I can't stop sneezing. It hurts!" He started to walk toward the frightened inmate.

The inmate got mad and smashed the officer with a plate of food in his face and said, "Maybe this will help you!" Then he moved away from the officer who started to bleed out from his eyes. The inmates that were in the dayroom ran to their cells and locked their doors behind them as the officer was charging at them screaming for help. Then he fell, hitting his head on the floor. He lay there unconscious in a pool of blood while the inmates looked in horror as the corrections officer defecated his internal organs.

Over at a nearby restaurant, the morning crowd kept the staff busy, especially the cook who was flipping pancakes, eggs, and bacon all at once. The owner of the restaurant was walking around, asking costumers if everything was okay and if they needed anything. When he approached a table at the end of the restaurant, there was a young couple having breakfast. He looked at them and started to act strangely. His eyes started to leak blood, and they popped out, landing inside the customers cup of coffee. The lady customer got up, screaming as the owner of the restaurant fell on the table with blood gushing out his mouth. The girl's boyfriend got up, horrified. The couple ran out of the restaurant along with other frightened customers and staff.

Victor arrived at his house with Abdul to pick up the RV, which was in the backyard. He told Abdul, "Okay, wait here. I'm going inside to get the keys to the RV."

"I got to take a shit."

"Very well, follow me." They both went inside, and Victor showed him where the bathroom was. Victor went to the backyard and turned on the RV. He then turned on the radio to a news station. "There is a nationwide manhunt for the terrorist who are responsible for poisoning thousands of people throughout the tristate area. The police believe Abdul Malik along with his accomplices Usman Mohammad and Zyan Alijaber are still in the area. There is a one-million-dollar reward for any information leading to the capture of these violent terrorist who are armed and dangerous. If you see them, please call your local police department."

Victor thought, "Wow, when they catch them, it's lights out for them. I should turn their asses in and claim that reward. But then again, they looking for me too. I got to make this money and leave to Mexico."

Abdul walked out of the bathroom and passed by Victor's son's room. He went inside and saw a picture of Victor's son on the dresser, standing in front of a university his son, Jason, attends. He grabbed the picture and put it in his pocket. Victor was in front of his son's room.

"What the hell you doing in here?"

Abdul turned around. He pointed to a picture on the wall, "That's your son?"

"Yea, come on let's get out of here."

Manhattan, New York City

Mohammed and Zyan were in the house praying. Zyan got up. "I'm going out to get something to eat. You want something?"

"I don't think it's a good idea going out."

"Don't worry about me, I could handle myself." Mohammed decided to go with him. When they got to the chicken place, Mohammad placed an order then sat down while Zyan went to the bathroom. Two police officers entered the fast food place. As they were placing their orders, a TV on the wall was broadcasting the people who were dying from the chemical attack and showing the faces of the terrorists.

Police Officer Mike Phillips and his partner Marshall Reed were looking, shaking their heads. "Wow, you see that?"

"Yea, I sure like to run into one of them. That bank robbery up in Delaware was a massacre. I got to go take a leak." He handed his partner a ten-dollar bill to cover for the food.

Mohammed got nervous. He was looking for his phone. "Where's my phone." He got up and went outside to the van to call Zyan who was in the bathroom in front of the mirror cleaning his hands. Reed came inside, and when Zyan saw him, he bent his head down to avoid being seen by the cop.

Reed started to urinate. He looked at Zyan as he was leaving and recognized his face. "Hey you, stop. Turn around." Zyan turned around with his gun out as Reed was reaching for his gun. Zyan shot Reed in the face and ran out the bathroom. Mohammad heard the gunshot and ran inside the chicken place. Officer Phillips also heard the gunshot and took out his gun. He saw Zyan running out the bathroom and told him to freeze. Zyan turned to shoot at Philips who returned fire, killing Zyan.

Mohammed took out his gun and shot at Officer Phillips, striking him in the arm and leg. The cop returned fire and hit the terrorist in the shoulder. As Mohammed tried to run out of the restaurant, Phillips shot him in the ass and in the back of his legs. Mohammed dropped to the floor and tried to crawl to his car. Officer Phillips limped to the bathroom and saw his partner dead on the floor. He called for an ambulance and for back up. He then limped outside and followed the blood trail to the suspects' car and saw him slumped over the steering wheel. He checked for his pulse and saw he was still alive. An employee who worked in the restaurant came running out. Phillips screamed to him to call for an ambulance.

When Abdul and Victor got to Zyan's house, he knocked on the door and there was no answer. Abdul turned the doorknob and opened the door. They entered the apartment, and Abdul started yelling, "Mohammed, Zyan, where the hell are you?"

Victor was looking at the TV. He saw Zyan's body covered in a white sheet and Mohammed who was on a stretcher, being put into an ambulance. Victor yelled to Abdul, "I found them!."

Abdul came in the living room, and Victor pointed to the TV. He told Abdul, "They must have gone to get something to eat and that cost them their lives." The news anchor was elaborating on the shootout that left the one terrorist dead along with a police officer. They showed the terrorists' faces and put Abdul's face on the screen. There was a massive hunt for him.

Abdul got mad and yelled, "These fools, I told them to wait for me here. They don't listen. That's good for their asses!"

Victor was getting nervous. He wanted to get away from Abdul before he got killed. He saw Abdul was all over the news and eventually would be hunted down. He went into the bathroom and looked out the window. He opened it and started to crawl out.

Abdul knocked on the door and asked Victor for the keys to start loading the drugs onto the RV. Victor put his leg back into the bathroom. He opened the door and handed Abdul the keys. Victor told him, "I be right out. I got to take a crap." Victor locked the door and climbed out the window. He ran across a yard, hopped a fence, and ran into another yard. Then he ran into the street and saw a bus coming. The bus stopped and he got on. As the bus driver was driving down the avenue, he started to bleed out from his eyes and sneezed blood out of his nose, covering the windshield with blood. He pressed the wiper button to try to see as his blood was smearing all over the windshield, causing him to crash into a crowed intersection killing pedestrians and other motorists. Victor crawled out of the bus and ran.

After Abdul loaded up the RV, he knocked on the bathroom door, and when he saw that Victor was not answering him, he broke the door down and saw Victor wasn't there. He screamed, "You want to play games!"

Victor's son was in his dormitory looking at the news. The news was broadcasting people dead on stretchers in the emergency room by the dozens. His father called him and told him to meet him in the front of the school in ten minutes. Jayden asked his dad, "Have you been looking at the news? There are people dying of blood leakage."

"Yea I'm sure glad you not a drug addict. I'll explain it to you when I see you."

Abdul went to Jayden's school. He had his picture in his hand and saw him in front of the university. Inside the school, two female college students were sniffing cocaine and then started experiencing the effects of the deadly drugs. In panic, they ran out the dorm in their panties and bras, passing Jayden who was stunned and scared as the females were rolling on the ground screaming for help. Blood was leaking out their eyes, mouths, and ears. Victor was in a cab that was stuck in traffic. When the cars started to move, the cab driver did not move his car. He was slumped over the steering wheel bleeding out from his nose and eyes. Victor got out the cab and looked at the cab driver, calling him a coke head.

Abdul blew the horn to the RV to get Jayden's attention. As Jayden approached the RV, Abdul pulled out his gun and told him to get in. Victor got to the front of the school since he did not see his son. He called him.

Jayden asked Abdul, "What do you want with me?" His phone started ringing.

Abdul asked, "Aren't you going to answer it?"

"It's my father."

Abdul snatched the phone from Jayden. He told Victor, "You think you smart you dumb spic."

"If you do anything to my son, I'm going to kill you."

"The only one who is going to die here is your son if you don't show up by the George Washington Bridge in a half an hour. Do you understand, Victor?" Abdul tied Jayden up then he takes out a bomb from his bag.

Jayden asked, "What are you going to do with that?"

"You'll see." He tied the bomb around Jayden's head and told him, "If I was you, I won't move too much unless you don't mind blowing up to smithereens."

As the RV passes a night club, there was a woman running out, holding her bleeding nose. She was screaming, "My nose, my nose, it hurts. Help me!" She tried grabbing a man walking down the street.

He said, "Get off me!" Then she ran into the street and a bus hit her. Inside the club, a girl was in the bathroom sniffing a bag of cocaine. She went out to the dance floor and started to dance with a guy. Then a burst of blood came out of her noise that got all over the guy she was dancing with. She started to scream, "I can't stop bleeding." Then she fell in the middle of the dance floor with blood gushing out her eyes and mouth. Everybody in the club started to freak out, running away from her.

Abdul was in Washington Heights by the George Washington Bridge waiting for Victor who was walking toward the RV. When Victor got in, Abdul searched him for any weapons. He asked, "Where's my son?" Abdul took Victor to the back and opened the door from the bathroom. There Victor saw his son with a bomb tied to his head. Victor turned around and said, "What, are you crazy!"

"You shouldn't run like a coward, and if you try to get slick again, I'm blowing him up." Abdul showed Victor a detonator he had in his hand. "If I push this bottom, I'm sending him to the moon. Now let's get back to the plan. Get on 95. We're heading down south."

Ken was at his office sitting by his desk and wondering where Abdul was. He was staring at the TV that was showing people who were either dead or dying on the streets of New York. At local hospitals, families of the dead victims demanded to know why their loved ones died of sudden blood loss. One doctor was explaining what could be causing it. People were worried if it was contagious. The doctors were saying the blood leakage was severe hypertension bleeding from the brain. The sneezing of the blood came from internal abnormalities, symptoms stemming from ruptured blood vessels, causing brain hemorrhage from arteries bursting in the brain and destroying the brain cells. As autopsies were performed on the dead bodies, high levels of toxic chemicals were a main factor of death. In explaining the blood leakage from the ears, otologists examined the bodies and conducted an otoscopic exam where an otoscope was inserted in the ears of the dead victims, discovering huge holes in their eardrums caused from a barotrauma where the pressure inside the ear was not equal to the pressure outside. It caused chronic pain, like when one was in a plane while it was rapidly descending or being a thousand feet underwater, a very painful encounter. Then there was the defecation of internal organs. In other terms, it was not a bowel incontinence but an organ incontinence, where according to gastroenterologists who concluded that the victims internal organs were forcibly and violently moved toward the rectum, falling under the clinical categorization of intestinum rectum. Before dying, the victims were going through tenesmus, the need to push out even when bowels were empty and organs started to be either defecated out by vomit or forced out the rectum. It caused harsh straining and painful cramping as the body became paralyzed and bled out.

A worried relative of a deceased asked, "Is there a cure?"

The doctor shook her head. "Yes, stay drug free."

It is apparent that the ingesting of drugs mixed with deadly chemicals were the primary cause of death.

One family member said, "But my daughter wasn't an addict."

The doctor answered, "I drink socially. Does that make me an alcoholic?"

Ken changed to another news channel. There was breaking news on a republican politician who was running for the presidency who was speaking in front of congress on national TV. All of a sudden, viewers witnessed a horrific mind-boggling disturbance when the old politician started gushing blood out of his nose then out of his ears and started to regurgitate his internal organs in front of millions of viewers.

Ken turned off the TV and shook his head in disgust he went to his parents' house, where he fell asleep on the couch. His mother came downstairs and got him a blanket. The next day, Ken's mother made breakfast for Henry and Ken. She told him, "What is this world coming to. All these people dying on the streets."

Henry said, "I hear terrorists are taking advantage of the weak, mainly addicts. If they accomplish that plot, you might be out of a job, son.".

Ken laughed. "That's how my commander feels."

Ken's mother asked him, "I remember when you were a cop on the beat. Now you're putting your life in danger to avenge your sister's death. Look at you. I don't know who you are anymore, son."

Ken grabbed a piece of bread and looked at his dad. He told his mother, "I know you and Dad worry. But if I don't do it, who will? What happened to Jessica was an injustice."

Henry said, "What your mother is trying to say is that she doesn't want to lose you like she lost Jessica."

Ken grabbed his mother's hand. "Mom, I'm not going anywhere. I promise you that I'm going to be safe. I have an army behind me."

Ken's mother replied, "And so did Jessica."

GEORGIA

Victor was driving the AV down the thruway 95. He got off and entered the Georgia 185 Thruway, arriving in a small town called Somer Lake. They stopped at a night club owned by one of Juan Carlos's main distributors. Abdul told Victor, "I'm going to let you go and negotiate by yourself. Dump fifty keys on him. Give him a good deal so he could flush that shit. Now I don't hear people dying in this neck of the woods, guess who's going to Mars."

Victor went inside and saw Troy by the bar adding up some receipts. "Hey, Troy, how's it going?"

Troy looked up and saw Victor. He got up and hugged him. "Wow, look what the wind blew in. Where the hell is everybody at? I've been calling Julio, and he don't pick up. Did he go on vacation again?"

"Julio is out of town, but he sent me."

"Sent you for what? I ain't givin' up no money until I talk to him."

"Relax, he sends you fifty keys."

Troy smiled. "Really, now we're talking. I got bread for Julio from the last load."

Victor told him, "Listen, I got a lot more of that shit. So try to unload it quick, okay?"

"You know me. I don't sit on nothing, man." Troy asked, "Is it the same shit?"

"Of course, cyanide." Victor went outside and got inside the RV. He told Abdul to pull out fifty bricks.

"That's what I want to hear."

Victor asked, "Can I see my son?"

Abdul opened the door to the bathroom, and Victor saw his son. He was sitting on the toilet with a bomb strapped around his head, sweating and in tears. Victor told him, "Don't worry, son, I got one more stop then this will be over. Just hold your head, I mean try to stay still, okay." Victor turned to Abdul. "Must you leave him in there tied up like that?"

"What you want me to do? You forced this on yourself by climbing out the bathroom window."

Victor took out a candy bar and hand fed his son. He told him, "Just chew slowly."

Troy's manager helped Victor with the load. He opened one of the bricks to check for the logo Cyanide with the stamp of a double-tailed scorpion. He went back to the office and showed his boss. Troy smiled. "We back in business. Go get the mix and put five hundred on each one."

Victor then went into Troy's office and saw stacks of money on the top of his desk. Troy asked, "You want to count it?"

"I trust you" and started to put the money into a duffel bag. Victor got back on the highway and headed for Miami. Back at the strip club, Troy had different workers coming to pick up various amounts of Abdul's spiked drugs to be distributed throughout the Georgia area.

An ambulance driver who bought some of the drugs and consumed it was bringing a sick person to the emergency room. The city worker started to react to the after effects and started to bleed out of his nose, eyes, and ears. As he was pulling up to the hospital, he started to lose his eyesight and crashed into the emergency room, mowing down sick patients and killing a half-dozen hospital staff.

A volleyball coach who was coaching a volleyball team started to bleed out from his nose and eyes. He was screaming for help and started to chase the college female volleyball players. They all ran in horror out of the gym. As the coach was running blindly, he ran into a pole and fell to the floor and died.

MANHATTAN

Ken was driving with Agent Romo to the hospital where Mohammad was recovering. When they got upstairs, they flashed their badges at a female officer who was sitting outside guarding the high profile prisoner. The agents entered the room and saw Mohammed resting on the bed.

Ken told him, "Hey, Mohamed, I'm glad they didn't kill you because now your miserable ass could tell me where Abdul is and what his next move is."

"I have nothing to say to you."

Ken told Romo to close the door. Then he pulled out two thin rubber hoses and asked Mohammed if he knew what they were for. Mohammed looked at the hoses.

"No, and I don't care." Ken then grabbed Mohammed by the back of his neck. Mohammed told him, "What are you doing?"

Ken started to duct-tape his mouth. He asked him, "Remember when I got my mouth duct-taped, do you remember these hoses your sick cousin stuck in my nostrils?" Ken pulled out a bag containing a powdery substance. "Do you remember this?" Ken told Romo, "Come and hold this piece of shit." The officer who was outside on duty came in the room. Romo turned around and blocked Ken. She asked if she could go to the bathroom and not to leave until she returned.

Romo told her, "Sure, take your time." Romo came and held the terrorist down as Ken stuck the rubber tubes into Mohammed's nose and duct-taped it to secure them in place. Then at the end of the tubes, Ken started to put in the white powder. He told Mohammed if he didn't tell him where Abdul was or his plans were, he was going to die like the rest of the addicts they poisoned. Mohammed's eye's started to enlarge as he was looking at the powder getting closer to his nostrils. He then started to shake his head up and down to indicate to Ken he knew were his cousin

Abdul was. When the agents left the hospital, Ken looked at Romo and said, "Looks like we're flying to Miami then to Canada."

Ken tossed the bag of the powder into the street. Romo said, "How about if somebody picks that up?"

Ken laughed. "It's all right. That's just baking soda." Both men started to laugh.

Miami

The RV reached Miami. Victor was at the marina, handing a group of men the last load of drugs to be disturbed throughout the Miami area. They were happy to see Victor who asked one of the men for a gun. The men divided the drugs and left in different cars. Within a few hours, a captain of a large yacht who recently sniffed sum of the poisonous powder started to react strangely. He was on deck with a female companion who also was getting high. Blood started to leak out of her nose and eyes. She was screaming that it hurt her and grabbed a towel, placing it on her nose trying to stop the bleeding. The pain was so excruciating that she was running blindly tripping and fallen over board. Blood started to spread in the water and within minutes, she drew a group of great white sharks to her who shredded her to pieces, devouring her within seconds. The captain of the boat was bleeding out of his eyes and could not see. His eyeballs popped out and got stuck to the boat's windshield. He crashed into the marina where dozens of people were eating outside on the deck and had fallen into the water, causing a frenzy with the hungry sharks. Also in the water was a little baby girl who was in the arms of her frantic mother that was screaming for help. As a great white shark was zeroing in on the helpless mother and child, it started opening its huge mouth full of razor sharp teeth, and just as it was about to devour them, a wave came across with a human body smashing in front of the hungry shark which snapped the man in two, disappearing underwater.

Abdul and Victor rode past the Miami Heat stadium. They drove till they got to a golf resort. Victor pulled up to the front. "Okay, Ab, I did everything you asked. Now free my son so we could get out of here."

"Sorry, there's been another change of plans. I need for you to drive me up to Canada then I'll free your son."

Victor started yelling, "What the hell, you keep changing your mind, I'm tired of your shit, man!"

"You ain't got no choice unless you want me to send your son passed the moon. Shut up and do as you're told. Now I got to go to the bathroom and don't be stupid and try to leave. I got the detonator in my hand."

Abdul left the RV and walked inside to use the bathroom. Victor opened the door to the bathroom where his son was. Tears were coming down the side of his face. Victor told him while crying, "Don't worry, son, I'm going to get you out of here right now. Victor exited the RV and went inside the golf resort. He entered the bathroom and heard Abdul singing in Arabic. Victor bent down and saw Abdul's sandals. He then kicked in the door and found Abdul on the toilet. He kicked Abdul in the face and put the gun to his mouth. He asked Abdul, "Where is it? Where is the detonator?"

Abdul was bleeding in his face as he held it up and said, "Boom."

Victor looked back when he heard a loud explosion outside. He screamed, "No!"

Abdul grabbed Victor's weapon. Both men started to wrestle with the gun and then it went off. People came running out the lounge area to see the RV on fire. A worker called the fire department and told them there was a truck burning.

Ken and Romo landed at the Miami international airport. They got a call and heard about the RV explosion. Agents from the Miami DEA picked up Ken and Romo, and they headed toward the golf resort.

When they got to the location, officers from the Miami Police Department were interviewing an employee who discovered a dead man in the bathroom. And another witness who saw an Arab running from the scene. When Ken went to inspect the body, he identified it as Victor Alvarez. Abdul was driving a golf cart away from the main lounge. He stopped and jumped a fence to a residential street. He walked down the block and saw across the street a woman getting out her car and entering her house. Abdul knocked on the door, and when the woman opened, Abdul shot her in the head. She fell back, hitting the floor. Abdul grabbed the keys to her car, got in, and drove off. Ken told the DEA agents from the Miami office to put a chopper in the air and surround the perimeter, expanded by a ten-mile radius. A Miami Police captain approached Ken and told him, "Strange things have been happening."

Ken asked, "Like what?"

Captain Malvaldo explained "A captain of a boat who rammed his yacht into a marina full of people was found with his eye sockets drenched in blood."

Ken said, "Really? Sounds like he was dipping in a little coke."

The captain said, "Say what?"

Ken instructed him to arrange a press conference and make the public aware that there was a terrorist on the loose who had contaminated a large quantity of drugs. "They must refrain from buying and consuming drugs if not face death."

The captain replied, "These drug addicts ain't going to stop.

Romo told the captain, "Then it's time to clean the city."

There was a national golf tournament going on, and a caddy rode a golf cart recklessly into a crowd of spectators, running over a few old people. He was found dead with blood dripping out his mouth, ears, nose, and eyes. Ken went past the Miami Stadium. There was a panic going on inside when a basketball player was shooting a free throw and started to sneeze blood out of his nose. And then blood started squirting out of his eyes and ears. He was screaming for help then started running toward his teammates. They were all in shock and frightened, and they were running away from him in fear. A vendor selling food, started to bleed out from his mouth and eyes. Massive blood was pouring onto the hotdogs like it was ketchup. He also threw up blood on the popcorn he was selling. Then he dropped the food and ran into the court, covering his eyes and crashing into the blind basketball player. Flooding the court with blood, teammates and fans were slipping on the slippery floor trying to exit the stadium. One fan was screaming "We are under attack. There are zombies attacking us!"

The Miami captain and the Miami DEA office along with the agents from the Anti Terrorism Taskforce were doing a press conference in front of the media. The captain was warning the public of a toxic drug that was killing thousands of people.

In a town a few miles up, a man was putting gas to his car. A car pulled up at the station and a man jumped out, screaming that his eyes were hurting as blood was gushing out of his mouth. He was holding a cigarette as he approached the man who was pumping gas. When the man saw the addict in front of him, he panicked and took out the gas hose from his car and started to pour in on the crazed man who bust into flames.

SYRIA

Avenda was in a house in Syria, filled with rebel fighters who were taking turns raping her. She was then transported to an orphanage where she was forced to take care of displaced children that the terror network were raising to become suicide bombers and jihadists. She was washing dirty clothes by hand and was forced to cook three times a day for more than two hundred starving kids. When she refused to have sex with the rebel guards in charge, she was beaten to near death. At night, she used to stare up into the sky and wondered how could she have abandoned her family back in the States for a life of torture and slavery. Many endless nights went by with her looking up at the stars praying to God for forgiveness. She used to think on how her friend Asma fought hard to stop her from making the dreadful mistake in taking that fatal trip to hell. It had destroyed her life and surely, her sick mother as well. Then one night, Avenda heard gunshots from automatic weapons outside. A group of militant women fighters from Syria, called the de facto army, stormed the camp and killed all the rebel guards. Amreen was leading the assault. She was part of a movement fighting against the opposition. Many of the children ran away from the camp. Amereen found Avenda and told her, "You have the choice to come with us or stay."

Avenda replied, "I'm tired of getting beaten and raped." Amereed grabbed her hand and escorted Avenda out of the camp and to safety. Avenda went to a safe house which was a hideout for the militant women fighters. Avenda told her how she got to the country to help the opposition. And it wasn't what they told her it would be. Instead, she felt she went to hell and wanted to kill herself. Eventually with the help of Amreen, she traveled back to the States and was reunited with her family and friends. When she saw Asma, she ran toward her, hugging her and telling her, "I'm sorry for trying to get you to go with me. You were right. I went under

---

false pretenses. I was forced to be a sex slave. There were young girls being sold for as little as thirteen dollars." Asma was in tears while listening to Avenda's tales of horror. "I don't know how I'm going to tell my parents that I am pregnant."

Asma said, "What, are you sure?"

"Yes, I am sure, Asma. Worse, I don't know who the father is because I was repeatedly raped by different men."

Canada

Abdul arrived in Canada undetected. He was met there by a Canadian terror network who provided a roof over his head while he planned to unleash another chemical attack. The leaders of the radical group were praising Abdul for the massacre he was responsible for back in the States. Abdul stood in front of a camera and started to record his propaganda, "To the people of the United States and the rest of the world, I, Abdul Malik, a self-proclaimed jihadist working under my Lord and Prophet have served and set out to destroy the infidels, the evil Westerners who have been oppressing my homeland for years. If you don't stop the drone attacks and occupation of the Middle East, I will continue to cause destruction to all my enemies. The body count is in the thousands and climbing. And what's chilling is that I'm preparing a another massive dosage to contaminate the food you eat and the water you drink. You the people must pressure your government to stop attacking my homeland and stop the drone strikes. If not, I will continue to infect up to the air you breath."

The one-minute video was posted on YouTube for the world to see. Ken was at the Canadian Airport with Romo, looking at the video clip that was broadcasting on TV around the world. A van from the Canadian Special Forces picked up Ken and Romo at the airport. They drove to the department's headquarters and quickly Ken gave a rundown on Abdul, his plans, and his possible location.

Abdul was staying in a house located in Gatineau, Canada, a densely wooded area surrounded by swamps. As the jeep Abdul was in approached a narrow path off the main road, the Canadian driver drove through a swampy road that led to a secluded cabin. The wolves could be heard howling at night. There, a group of young Canadian radical rebels helped Abdul bring in all sorts of boxes full of laboratory equipment and drums of different liquid chemicals he needed to produce another deadly batch of a liquid that he would use to spray fields of Canibus plants to poison them. Abdul told the group he wanted to ship the contaminated grass back to the States and wipe out all the potheads. The senior leader of the terrorist group told Abdul he had transportation connections that could get the spiked weed to Arizona and Texas.

Ken was on his way with a team of heavily armed police men from the Canadian Drug and Terrorist Task Force to a remote address Abdul gave Mohammed to meet up in case they were ever separated.

After Abdul completed his complex, lethal mix, he went outside to the back of the house where they were seven foot cannabis plants. He sprayed them with his mixture and stripped a bud from the plant. He then waited for it to dry. "Whoever smoke this, their lungs are going to disintegrate."

Ken and the special forces were a few miles away from where Abdul was staying. Abdul was driven into town where he stopped at a local school. He found a young kid by the name of Joey and quickly became his friend. They were at the back of the schoolyard when Abdul asked him if he knew how to roll.

Joey said, "I sure do." Abdul took out a bud, and the kids eyes grew large. "Wow, that's a nice size, bud." He crushed it and rolled it. Abdul took out another bud that wasn't spiked and asked him to roll it for him. Once the kid rolled it, Abdul told him, "You smoke your own joint, and I smoke my mine."

Joey said, "Hey, what ever you say. The kid lit up his joint and passed the lighter to Abdul who lit his up but did not inhale the smoke. As Joey inhaled the deadly smoke, he started choking, saying, "This stuff is good." Then he fell off the bench and onto the ground, grabbing his throat. He told Abdul, "Something strange is happening."

Abdul asked, "Really, like what?" Joey kept choking, and then he started to throw up. Blood started to spill out of his mouth and then he slowly defecated his heart and lungs out. He died quickly. Abdul said, "Man, that is a messed--up way to die." Abdul was driven back to the cabin. He started spraying all the plants. Abdul and his accomplices placed hundreds of pounds into boxes that were bound for the USA. Afterward, Abdul mixed more drugs and went to another Cannabis field where there were hundreds of plants. He heard a chopper and ran for cover.

Ken and the other agents finally reached their destination and were closing in on Abdul who ran into the cannabis garden. Ken was speaking through a loudspeaker "It's over. Surrender, Abdul, we have the place surrounded!" Abdul's radical friends engaged in a shootout with Ken and the Canadian Police. Abdul kept running through the weed fields, firing his weapon at Ken and Romo who split up as they were chasing him. Ken got lost in the fields and wound up back by his truck. He was upset that once again, Abdul was nowhere to be found. Ken grabbed a gas mask and put it on. He told all the other police to get out of the fields and put on a gas mask. They stopped shooting at the Canadian rebels who were still hiding in the weed fields. Ken lit up a cannabis plant that spread rapidly to the rest of the field. The toxic smell filled the air. Abdul's accomplices started to inhale the deadly fumes. They painfully died, vomiting out their insides that was visible in plain site as smoke was coming out of them. The Canadian Police called in the fire department to put out the fire. When the Fire Hazmat team came in to search for bodies, they found ten of Abdul's men and Agent Romo dead with no mask on. Abdul had killed him and took his mask. His heart, lungs, and intestines, which he defecated, were gruesomely lying by his side.

When Ken found Romo, he screamed, "You're not going to get away, Abdul Malik. I'm going to hunt you down you coward!"

Ken's screams echoed throughout the Canadian mountains as Abdul hid in a cave away from the Canadian Aerial SWAT team. Ethan Logan was head of CBA, the Canadian Bounty Association, a group of men who specialized in hunting fugitives. A Special Tactical SWAT team was also involved in the manhunt. Ken asked Logan, "What are his chances of surviving up there?"

"Not much. If the wolves don't get him, there are hungry grizzly bears roaming those mountains. Probably find him frozen in one of those caves up there."

The noise of a rattle snake woke Abdul up. He was cuddled up in a fetal position. His feet and fingers were numbed from the freezing temperatures. He knew he had to be on the move before the police zeroed in on his location. As he approached the entrance of the cave, the sunlight blocked his vision. When he was able to get his sight back, there was a pack of hungry wolves staring at him outside the cave. Abdul made a run for it. He ran as fast as he could down a steep hill with the pack of wolves behind him. He tripped and fell, finding himself surrounded by the wild animals that were growling at him. One of the wolves leaped out at Abdul. He fired one round from his weapon, killing the predator which landed on him. The other wolves scattered when they heard the gunshot. Abdul got up and kept running until he ran out of breath. He dropped to the ground from exhaustion. He started to cry, "My God, please don't let me die out here." He leaned against a tree and fell out. A while later, he was awakened from the poop of an eagle dropping on his forehead. He got up and saw a nine-hundred-pound grizzly bear staring at him. Abdul grabbed his AK-47 and squeezed the trigger. But there were no bullets left in the magazine. Abdul got up and ran for his life. The bear chased him all the way to the edge of a mountain. Abdul looked down and saw a river three hundred feet down. He turned and saw the bear closing in on him. The bear was three feet in front of him, standing on its two feet and hovering over Abdul. The beast was over seven-feet tall, roaring at Abdul. It swung its huge paw, hitting Abdul on the shoulder and causing him to fall over the cliff. Bounty hunters heard the screams of a man as Abdul hit the water.

A month went by with no sign of Abdul. Ken was dreaming about what his partner Romo told him, "Ken we have to go after all of them, and cut off the heads off all the snakes. Or else they going to keep on poisoning our streets. At least Los Bandidos, who were directely responsible for Jessica, Muller and Sammy's death. "I think about it every moment of my life." "Your my partner and friend and like a brother to me. I will be with you till the end no matter what. I will not let nothing happen to you. You know word on the street is, after you killed the leader of the Los Hermanoes Ferte Jaun Carlos Santos, and his top lieutenant Julio Mendez, the Columbian Cartel Los Banditos vowed to hunt you and your family down." Ken started moaning and sweating. The dream he was having with Romo turned into a nightmare when he dreamed that the Columbian Cartel went to his parents house and butchered them alive. Also finding Lulu hung by her tail from the ceiling fan with her head chopped off. Ken was drenched in sweat screaming, No! Ken woke up and unzipped his tent. He crawled out and packed his tent. He looked up and saw an eagle flying over him. He took a comb out of his knapsack and combed the long beard he grew. He promised Jessica, Lynda, and Romo he would not cut it off until Abdul was either captured or killed. He hiked to the end of a mountain and picked up a ripped sleeve from a shirt. He pulled out his binoculars and looked down from the cliff to the roaring river. He screamed, "Abdul, where the hell are you!"

Printed in the United States
By Bookmasters